Choppy Waters

Part Two in

The Ugliness Trilogy

I0677193

John U. Gunter

ISBN: 0-692-13693-2
ISBN-13: 978-0-692-13693-5 (JoGun Publishers)

1

Chloe lay belly-down on the beach, her skin baking in the warm sun, wishing that somehow it could warm her frigid heart as well as her backside. She'd been here in Cancun for a little over a week but had found no escape from the ache inside her gut, which seemed to grow by the day. She missed Peter worse than she could have ever imagined missing anyone. Looking to her left and down the beach, she could see her friend, Rebecca, playing in the sand with Barry. The sight of Barry frustrated her. Deep inside her dying heart she knew that her little boy was not to blame for her husband's death. Peter's life had been taken by an unhinged lunatic. No one could have seen it coming. The haunting compulsion to blame Barry's behavior for the sad state of their now-broken family turned her stomach.

Snapping out of her negative thoughts, she turned her gaze to the right and searched the sands for Mila. The sight of her daughter's frail figure coming down the beach gave her pause—she was scanning the beach for her mother. Chloe became alarmed as the girl began running full speed toward her, yelling, "Mommy, Mommy!" Standing quickly, Chloe ran to meet her. She grabbed Mila and searched her for wounds, then relaxed and let Mila catch her breath.

Chloe asked, "What's the matter, sweetie?"

Mila panted, and said, "I saw aunt Gracie."

Chloe shook her head. She said, "That's impossible, sweetheart. Grace has been missing for years."

"I'm almost for sure it was her, Mommy. You have to come look before she leaves."

"Where is she?"

"She's way over there." Mila pointed to a couple sitting in beach chairs.

Chloe sighed. She said, "Okay. Let's go look. We're just going to walk by close enough to see, though. I don't want to be bothering anyone."

"Yes, let's go. I was so little the last time I saw her, but I know you'll know for sure."

Chloe took Mila's hand and glanced back over to Rebecca and Barry. Barry was busy burying Rebecca in sand. She shook her head and headed in the direction of the couple. The thought that Grace could be alive and well made Chloe's heart flutter. She felt a slight glimmer of hope.

2

As they approached the couple, Chloe felt the thump in her chest quicken. She could see that the woman had short burgundy hair. A lump of disappointment rose in Chloe's throat. She thought how young Mila had been when she had last seen Grace. *Her mind must be playing tricks*, Chloe thought, and then—she saw the woman's face. It was Grace!

About the time Chloe moved directly in front of her, the woman picked up a sun shield and Chloe could hear her talking to the man in the chair beside her. She said, "Let's get off the beach, baby. I've had enough sun for one day."

The voice belonged to Grace. Chloe knew it. She approached the couple with Mila attached at her hip. Chloe said, "Grace. I know it's you."

Grace lowered the shade. She said, "I don't know what you're doing here, Chloe. I'm not going back."

The man beside her said, "Who is this, Courtney? Why is she calling you Grace?"

Grace turned to the man. She said, "Don't worry about them, Samuel. They're about to be on their way."

Samuel didn't look pleased. Grace said, "Where are

you staying, Chloe? I'll come by and we'll have a talk."

Mila broke from Chloe's side and ran to embrace Grace. Mila said, "It's been so long! We were all worried."

Grace hugged Mila. She said, "I know it, short stuff."

Chloe's heart broke, hearing that term of endearment used with Mila. Peter had called her short stuff. It affected Mila also and tears spilled down her little cheeks. Mila said, "My daddy's dead, Aunt Gracie. We're running away, too. It's okay. We forgive you."

Grace had to wipe her eyes. She looked at Samuel. She said, "Baby. I've got to take a walk with them. I'll meet you back at the hotel."

Samuel grunted. He said, "I want to know what's going on, Courtney. Who are these people?"

Grace reached over and touched his shoulder. She said, "I'll tell you. I promise. In the room, later, please."

Samuel shook his head. He said, "Always a mystery with you. Okay, go on. I'll meet you in the room in an hour or so."

Grace stood and took Mila's hand. They walked down the beach, leaving Samuel to himself.

3

Out of ear shot from Samuel, Grace turned to Chloe. She said, "I want to tell you everything, but not in front of Mila."

Chloe said to Mila, "Go with Rebecca, sweetie."

Mila sighed. She said, "I'm a big girl. I can hear."

Grace knelt down. She said, "It's adult stuff, shorty. I promise we'll spend time afterwards. I don't want you to have to think about the things I'm going to tell your mommy."

Mila frowned and started walking in Rebecca's direction. Grace stood and looked Chloe in the eyes. She said, "Kevin beat me after I last saw you, Chloe, as soon as we returned home."

Chloe ached inside, hearing her friends tone, imagining what she must have gone through. She said, "You didn't have to vanish, Gracie. You could have come to me."

"No. I thought the safest thing would be to disappear. He told me he'd kill me if I left him. He said they'd never find my body. The way he said it—the venom in his words—I felt I couldn't bring my problems anywhere near my friends. I thought it would be best if I left and told no one. Just start a new life."

"What about Darla? Aren't you worried about what he might do to her?"

Tears spilled down Grace's cheeks. She bit her index fingernail. She said, "I don't think he would hurt her."

"You don't believe that, Grace. I know you too well. You're worried he might hurt her."

Grace lowered her hand. Tears spilled freely. Chloe said, "We have to get her, Grace. We have to tell the police why you left and get Darla from that monster."

4

Rebecca watched from across the beach as Chloe talked to the woman she'd only seen in pictures. Sand filled every crevasse, but it was more than the grains of the beach making her feel uncomfortable. A feeling rose in the pit of her stomach. One Rebecca rarely felt. It was jealousy. Analyzing herself, Rebecca concluded that she feared this 'old' friend was a threat. She knew how much Chloe loved Grace.

Rebecca said to Mila, "Baby, let's go to the hotel and shower."

Overhearing the conversation, Barry moaned, "I'm still playing, Aunt Becca."

Rebecca smirked at him and ruffled his hair. She said, "I guess we could take a dip in the ocean really quick. I've got to get some of this sand off me."

The three of them headed for the water and Rebecca glanced back at Chloe and Grace. They were going in the direction of the hotel. Rebecca's ears heated up and she could feel herself flush. Sand squished in her toes and the tide rolled in, warming her digits. She took the hands of the children and headed further in until she could sit down and get some of the grime off.

She looked at Mila and then to Barry. She said, "I don't want to stay out here any longer. Let's go to the hotel for a while."

Barry sighed. He said, "Okay, Aunt Becca."

Mila asked, "Can we come back out in a little while? I want to play some more."

"Sure, honey. We can come out after a while."

Mila beamed and the trio headed for the hotel. Rebecca felt tension in her neck and silently chided herself for getting worked up. The closer they came to the hotel, the hotter her skin felt. An internal alarm was ringing in her skull and she had a premonition that the appearance of the lost friend was going to be a bad thing.

Entering the suite, goosebumps rose on Rebecca's skin. She looked at the children and could see they had goosebumps too. A glance at the thermostat revealed that someone had programmed it to 60 degrees. Rebecca set it at 70 and headed for the bathroom to get them all towels. When she reached for the bathroom doorknob, she found it locked. She could hear Chloe and Grace talking lightly on the other side. After a couple of taps on the door she heard shuffling. Rebecca knew they had to be up to something.

Chloe called out from the other side of the door, "Just a minute."

A few moments later Chloe unlocked the door and opened it. Rebecca stood in shock. Chloe and Grace both looked puzzled by Rebecca's facial expression.

Chloe asked, "What is it, Becca?"

Rebecca said, "Let's go in the bathroom."

Chloe stepped aside and let her in. She said, "What's going on, Becca?" Rebecca closed the door. She said, "I wanted to ask you the same thing."

"Nothing. I found Grace. Well, Mila found her. Why are you looking at me like that?"

Rebecca looked from Chloe to Grace and then back. She was mad enough to grit her teeth and from the vibe of the room the two women could perceive her aggravation. Rebecca took a deep breath and steadied herself. She looked at the counter and shook her head.

Chloe said, "You're acting real weird, Becca."

Rebecca asked, "What is that white ring around your nose?"

Chloe looked in the mirror. She said, "Oh my God."

Chloe turned on the faucet and washed the residue from the dirty nostril.

She said, "It's nothing, Becca."

"It doesn't look like nothing."

"We're just having a little fun. No big deal. I haven't seen Grace in forever."

Grace asked, "Why are you answering to this woman, Chloe?"

Rebecca started towards her and Chloe stood in between them. She knew what Rebecca was capable of and her tall and mouthy friend had no idea what she was getting into. The tension in the air was palpable. Chloe considered Rebecca's eyes and could see frustration festering in them.

Chloe said, "Grace, Rebecca is very important to me."

She turned to face Grace. Chloe said, "I think we

should apologize."

Rebecca retrieved three towels from the wall hanger, moving calmly and confidently. She said, "No need to apologize, Chloe. I'm not your boss, I'm your friend. I think it's a bad idea to use drugs or get involved with anyone with a habit. I've got to bring the kids towels, I suggest you get high somewhere else."

Rebecca turned without waiting for a reply and left the bathroom.

Grace said, "Your girlfriend is a real downer."

Chloe began to fidget. She said, "You don't know her, Grace. She's been helping me through a lot. She and the kids are all I've had to keep me sane after Peter's murder. You would like her if you got to know her. You're going to get to know her. Right?"

"I don't know, Chloe. If it was just you and me…I don't know if I can handle a boss. Don't roll your eyes, Chloe. She seemed intense."

"Just tell me you're not going to vanish. Tell me we're going to get Darla."

Grace breathed deeply and exhaled loudly. She said, "I'm not going anywhere. I have to talk to Samuel."

"I'll come with you."

"No. I have to talk to him alone. You still trust me don't you?"

"I do."

"Okay. I'll be back in a couple of hours."

"Why so long?"

"I'll have to pack my things. Won't I?"

"We can get you new things. Can't you just call him?"

"No. I have to see him in person. I owe him that much. There's a lot to tell him."

"He's an old man, Grace. Why are you with him?"

"He may be graying and balding, but he's a good man, Chloe. I want to leave the relationship on good terms."

"Do you love him?"

"No, I don't know if I'm capable of loving another man again."

"You love me, right?"

Grace leaned and hugged Chloe. She said, "I'll always love you, short stuff."

A dull pain rose in Chloe's chest. Peter's words from the lips of her long-lost friend. A tear escaped her eye and she closed her eyelids tight, wishing the embrace would never end.

Chloe said, "You hurry back. I'll talk to Rebecca while you're gone."

5

Grace and Chloe exited the bathroom and Mila ran to Grace. She asked, "Are you going to hang out with us? I missed you."

"I've got to go for now. I'll be back later and we can hang out."

Mila frowned. She asked, "You're coming back, right?"

Grace looked at Chloe then back to Mila. She said, "I'll be back."

"Okay. Because we didn't get to hang out. You have to hang out with me. I'm bigger now. I'm more fun."

Grace knelt to be at eye level with Mila. She said, "I'm sure you are, short stuff. I'll be back before you know it."

"Alright. I'll be waiting."

Grace left the room and Rebecca walked up and smiled at Chloe. She asked, "Do you think we can have a talk in private?"

Chloe knew Rebecca was in a foul mood. She followed Rebecca into the bathroom. When the door was closed, Rebecca crossed her arms and glared. Chloe sat on the edge of the bathtub. She wasn't sure what to say to her friend. She looked at the floor tiles, then to

Rebecca.

She said, "You look sexy all mad with that little hip cocked to the side. I like that bikini on you."

"Don't be funny, Chloe. What kind of role model can you be to the kids on drugs?"

"Damn, Becca. It's not like I'm an addict. I've done drugs before."

"Not with me you haven't."

"Well, I was just trying to have a good time with my friend. It's no big deal."

Rebecca sat next to Chloe and took her hand. She said, "It is a big deal, baby. That shit will fuck you up. I know."

"Have you used before?"

"No. My mother was a drug addict. You don't want Barry and Mila to look at you the way I looked at her."

"You've never talked about your mother before."

"I don't like to talk about her much, baby. She chose a life of drugs and God knows what else over a life with me and my father. It's no good, baby. We're going to have a good life together. Using dope can screw it all up. Can't you see? You've already been taking way too many pills. The last thing you need is to get hooked on illegal narcotics."

"I'm not getting hooked on anything, Becca. I was just trying it out. I haven't done cocaine since high school."

"Yeah, but it starts with a line and ends with a needle in your arm. Is that how you want to end up? I identified my mother's body after a drug overdose when I was eighteen."

"That's not how I'll end up, Becca."

"You don't know that. No one means to end up that way. Just tell me you won't use again. It's bad news. You already pop too much Xanax and sleeping pills."

"I need those. You know I do."

"Baby, I just don't want you using cocaine."

Chloe felt wretched inside. She didn't want to lie to Rebecca. Fidgeting and biting her lip, she sighed. She asked, "What are the kids doing?"

"The kids are fine. Please, don't try to avoid this conversation. I only want what's best."

"I'm not making any promises, Becca."

"Fair enough. I guess I'll have to have a talk with your friend."

"Don't do it. Don't drive her away." Tears filled Chloe's eyes. "I want her to come stay with us and go back to the states to get her daughter. You'd love her, Becca. You just have to get to know her."

Rebecca said, "She can come with us, baby. I'm not trying to drive anyone away, Chloe. I just think she needs to understand that I don't want anyone using drugs or carrying them around me or the children. You know I'm going to support you in *almost* anything you decide to do." Rebecca left the bathroom, leaving Chloe to think.

6

When Chloe left the bathroom, Rebecca was reading to the children. Chloe went to the dresser and put on some jogging pants. Inside she knew that Rebecca truly wanted what was best for her and the children. She knew she should have told Rebecca what she wanted to hear and she should want to say it and mean it. Not knowing what she wanted made it hard to make a definitive statement. Although she also knew the right thing to do would be to avoid destructive behavior, her soul was aching and hollow from the loss of Peter. He had been everything to her and without him she didn't want to be strong. She wasn't sure she wanted to be sober either.

Rebecca asked, "Are you going somewhere?"

Chloe bit her lip. She said, "I'm going for a walk on the beach."

Mila said, "We'll come with you, Mommy."

Chloe began fidgeting. She said, "I'd like to go alone, sweetie. Is that okay, Becca? I won't be long."

Rebecca said, "Baby, you do what you want. We're going back out on our own in a little while anyway."

Chloe said, "I'm sorry, Mila. Mommy just needs some alone time."

Barry interjected, "We miss him, too, Mama. It's okay."

Chloe's heart wrenched. Barry hardly brought up his father and she knew he blamed himself. Sometimes she couldn't help blaming him. If he hadn't brutally attacked the killer's son, then the man wouldn't have come after Peter. She found it hard to look at Barry at times because of the incident that sparked the fury of the madman who claimed the life of her beloved. The thought of Peter's blood splattered on her face and the killing of the innocent man that she thought had shot Peter kept her up at night if she didn't take the pills Dr. Blanch prescribed her. Chloe turned and walked out the door before she had a chance to say something she would regret to her five-year-old terror of a baby boy.

Outside the room, she wondered how long she would be able to hold the aggression she felt for Barry inside. Walking on the beach calmed her nerves, but she felt she needed more—like someone else to confide in. She wanted to talk to Grace. Rebecca had become a dear friend and even the reason she could hold it together as well as she had been, but seeing her long lost friend brought back memories of when she and Peter first became a couple. Grace knew her well, although she had vanished without a trace. The thought of her vanishing again made Chloe's stomach turn.

Grace had told her where she was staying and it was just a short walk up shore. Chloe decided she would go see how things were going with Samuel and try to help her get her things. The closer she got to Grace's hotel, the more her nerves stirred, giving her tremors. There was a wooden bench in front of the hotel, and Chloe took a seat there, debating on whether she was doing the right thing. The sun was setting and the view was spectacular. She knew Rebecca was probably on the beach with the children. Breathing in the warm sea air, Chloe closed her eyes and calmed herself.

She was abruptly interrupted from her relaxation by a guy's voice. He said, "Hello, gorgeous. You waiting on someone?"

Chloe opened her eyes to peer at the man in disapproval. She said, "No. I was just sitting here minding my business. I think you should do the same."

"We'll, that's an odd way to ask me to sit with you, but okay."

The guy sat next to her and Chloe became thoroughly annoyed. It was obvious to her that this guy was going to say something ridiculous. He looked to be in his early twenties, with kind of a surfer vibe to him, his wavy, blonde hair going everywhere. Attractive—but his attention was unwanted.

He said, "I'm about to score."

Chloe cocked her head to the side. "Excuse me?"

"Oh, I don't mean with you. That would be nice, don't get me wrong. I mean I'm about to get some shit. You wanna get high?"

Chloe showed him her ring finger. The rock Peter had placed there on their wedding day glistened in the lowering sun. Chloe said, "I'm married. Why don't you scram before my husband shows up and kicks your ass?"

The guy shook his head. He said, "Damn. Alright then. I'll be going."

When he stood to leave, Chloe had to hold back her tears. She wished with the whole of her soul that Peter was truly meeting her on the little wooden bench.

7

Chloe gained her composure and headed into the hotel to see Grace. Approaching the door to Grace's room, she paused. Having second thoughts she turned to leave. The door opened and she heard Samuel's voice. He said, "Hey—you're Grace's friend. Right?"

Chloe turned to face him and to her surprise the guy from the bench was standing with him. The guy said, "Alright, Sam. I'll see you next time."

He grinned when he walked past Chloe. Something about his grin made her skin crawl. It was apparent that Samuel was his dealer. Grace poked her head around Samuel. She said, "We were supposed to meet at your place, Chloe. What happened?"

"I just wanted to see you. Are you almost ready?"

"I will be. You didn't give me much time. Do you want to come inside while I get the rest of my things together?"

Chloe hesitated. She began fidgeting. Grace said, "It's okay. You don't have to."

Chloe shook her head. She said, "No. I want to. If you don't mind."

"Come on in, short stuff."

The room was dim and it wasn't hard to see that the couple partied hard. Half full and empty bottles of liquor covered the dresser top. At the desk, there was a mirror with cocaine residue. She could see Grace's bags were on the bed being packed. Chloe felt a sense of relief that Grace had been packing already.

Grace asked, "Do you want a line?"

Chloe shook her head. She said, "I don't think so. I was wondering if we could take a walk. Maybe have a talk."

"Sure. Do you want to wait until I pack my things? We could get a short cab to your place, then go for a walk. How's that sound?"

Chloe fidgeted and bit her lip. She said, "That's fine. Or we could just go for a walk and stay here when we get back."

"Oh, trouble in paradise?"

"Stop, Grace. It's not like that. Me and Becca are just friends."

"Could have fooled me. The way you two are. What's a girl to think?"

Chloe shook her head. She said, "She's been helping me through a real rough time and I love her, just like I love you. I hope you both can find a way to get along. If for no other reason than me and the kids love you both."

"I'll do my best, short stuff. As for staying here, I don't think it's a good idea. Samuel is very private. Unless you want to sleep with him? We've never done a threesome together." Grace laughed. It was the sound of a child laughing at a joke that started in her own head.

Chloe looked over at Samuel and the older graying male smiled and waved. Chloe said, "You know I just lost Peter, Gracie. I'm not sleeping with anyone."

Grace touched Chloe's shoulder. She said, "It was a joke, Chloe. I don't want to stay here because it's hard enough to leave now. If I stay much longer, I'll stay forever."

Chloe didn't know if she believed that Grace's statement was a joke. Breathing deep and trying not to look at Samuel, she gathered her composure. She said, "I don't want any drugs, but I'll take some alcohol. What do you have?"

Samuel spoke for the first time since he opened the door. He said, "We've got scotch. Or I could make you a White Russian."

"I'll take a scotch straight up." Something about having a drug dealer mix her a drink didn't settle right with Chloe.

Grace sat down on the small couch on the far side of the room and grinned. She asked, "How much did you miss me, Chloe?"

"We'll talk about that when we go for our walk later." Chloe took her scotch from Samuel and drew a swig.

Grace said, "I don't know if I'm comfortable being with your friend. She doesn't seem to like me much. How does she feel about me coming along?"

"She thinks you're a bad influence."

Samuel laughed. The sound was like gravel under tread. He said, "Courtney or Grace or whatever her name is happens to be the worst influence I've ever met."

He winked at Chloe and Grace stood. She said, "Oh, shut up, Sammy. You're just rotten."

She flipped him the bird and started to finish packing with the same silly grin on her face. Chloe wondered what might be going through her friend's head. She had no idea what Grace had been through or who she became. There was no way in her mind that she would willingly walk away and lose her again, but something grinding in the back of her consciousness told her that Rebecca was right: Grace was going to be trouble. The pressing question for her was, *what kind of trouble?*

8

Rebecca sat in the bathroom and brushed Mila's hair. Barry had fallen asleep in the plush bed almost an hour ago, and now seemed like a good time for some one-on-one time with the little girl whose light seemed to be dimming lately. Mila hid it well, but Rebecca could see Mila was falling apart behind the loss of her father. Not wanting to be pushy and upset the child, Rebecca brushed silently, thinking of the fact that her lawyer had recently drawn up the necessary paperwork to adopt Mila and Barry. Soon the little wonders who had been spending day and night by her side would be her legal children.

Mila said, "I don't think my mommy loves us the same."

Rebecca asked, "What do you mean, baby? Your mommy's just hurting. She still loves you. "

"I know she still loves me. It's just not the same. Did you know that she used to sing to me and with me sometimes? Not all the time, but sometimes she did. I feel like she will never sing with me again and I think she hates Barry. I see the way she looks at him. I'm pretty sure it's hate."

"That's not true, baby. She doesn't hate your brother. She's mad about what happened and I'm sure she blames him a little, but I don't think she hates him. He was trying to protect you. I'm sure that counts for something in your mother's eyes."

"I don't know, Aunt Becca. She isn't the same."

"We never are after life screws with us. None of us are, baby. Your mommy will be fine and you have me. I love you both so much. We're all going to be just fine. You have to roll with the blows and get up every time life knocks you down or it will run you over until you're dead. Don't let anything kill your spirit, baby girl."

"I do my best, Aunt Becca. I don't cry in front of her or nothing." Mila's eyes teared up when she turned to look at Rebecca. She said, "I lost him too, you know. It's like she doesn't even care how I feel."

Rebecca hugged Mila and they heard the front door open.

9

Chloe and Grace didn't enter quiet as church mice. They talked noisily, and Rebecca exited the bathroom with haste to quiet them down. The women looked at each other like they were all about to be involved in a showdown. Rebecca cocked her hip and squinted her eyes.

She said, "The little one is sleeping." In a hushed tone.

Chloe said, "We're here so I can get a top. It's getting chilly on the beach and we want to have a walk and talk for a while."

"We'll probably be sleeping before long, Chloe."

"Don't worry. Grace was able to get a room here. We can sleep there."

Rebecca sighed. She felt like she was losing Chloe. Not wanting to make her jealous feelings obvious and drive her further away, she calmed herself. She said, "Whatever you want, baby. We'll be here."

Chloe put a sweater on and left quickly. Mila said, "I told you. She doesn't care. Now that aunt Gracie is around it's just gonna get worse."

Rebecca turned to Mila with a curious look in her eyes. She said, "We can only control ourselves, baby.

Sometimes we can't even do that very well. Don't worry about your mommy. She'll find her way right to where she needs to be."

10

Chloe and Grace walked along the beach breathing in the night air and marveling at the stars and bright shining moon. Grace said, "We don't have to talk about anything if you don't want to. We can just walk along in silence, short stuff."

Chloe teared up. She said, "I want to talk about it. I need to. I need to tell you everything."

"Okay. I'm listening."

"After you left, on the night Barry bit Darla and Peter almost fought Kevin, I knew you were going to have to fight with Kevin. I didn't think he would end up beating you, I'm sorry for that. I just want to blame Barry for everything bad that's ever happened. He does so much bad shit, and over the years he's just gotten worse."

"Honey, you can't sit back and blame a five-year-old for all of our problems. Kevin was a piece of shit way before Barry bit Darla. I told you I was thinking of getting a divorce before that happened. That he was mean and aggressive. That's not Barry's fault."

"Wel—Mila was having boy problems at school. Some older kid bothering her. Being weird. When the boy pushed Barry to the ground after defending Mila,

27

Barry returned to the school with a rock in a sock and broke the kid's jaw. They'd never had a five-year-old do something like that. Barry was suspended, then the kid's father showed up at Peter's work and tried to fight him behind it."

"I see where you're coming from, Chloe. It's still on that guy."

"Are you serious? That *monster* shot my poor Peter right in front of us all! My husband's blood covered my face! I shot an innocent man thinking he was the asshole that shot Peter!" Tears spilled down Chloe's cheeks and she began trembling. "Are you telling me that all of this isn't that little shit, devil-bastard, son of mine's fault?! I'll never forgive him! Never!"

Grace embraced Chloe. She said, "Honey. Hating your son won't bring Peter back."

Chloe pushed away from Grace. She said, "You don't defend him. It's his fault. The man that shot Peter only got forty years, Grace. He might only have to do twenty. He's not much older than me. He'll be in his fifties walking around like nothing happened while my husband is rotting in the ground. It's not fair."

Chloe began walking up shore towards the resort hotel. Grace walked behind her for a way then jogged up beside her. She said, "How about a drink? The bar by the hotel has good margaritas."

"That's what you have to say?"

"I don't know what to say, honey. You've gotta help me out here. Cut me some slack."

Chloe stopped and wiped her eyes. Grace said, "I

don't always know what to say, honey. I'm sorry."

"It's not your fault. I thought I'd feel better if I talked about it. I haven't told anyone how I feel about Barry. I wanted to leave them both behind when Peter first got murdered. Am I a horrible person?"

"No, Chloe. You're grieving. I know how much you loved Peter. What he meant to you. I can hardly imagine what you must be going through inside."

"A margarita sounds good." Chloe bit her lip. She said, "Do you mind if I get sloshed and crash in your room?"

"Honey, I don't mind at all. Let's go get wasted."

11

Rebecca collected all the things that had been accumulated for everyone over the course of their stay. She was upset that Chloe didn't come back the night before and glad that the children were still sleeping while she had her coffee and packed. A glance at her watch revealed the time to be eleven fifteen. The late checkout was for one o'clock and it was frustrating that Chloe was being so irresponsible. Rebecca loved the kids, but she didn't like being treated like the babysitter.

Mila stirred and when Rebecca turned to look, she found the young girl smiling and looking at her. Mila asked, "Can you speak Chinese, Aunt Rebecca?"

Rebecca couldn't help but to smile at how adorable the nine-year-old princess was. She asked, "Is that it? No good morning, just straight to the interview?"

Mila yawned and covered her mouth. She said, "Good morning. Do you speak Chinese?"

"Well. I'm not Chinese, Mila. I'm Vietnamese and Italian."

"I had a dream that we were in some other country and you were speaking Chinese to someone. I was older. It was just you and me on vacation or something and you were buying something from someone. I wish I didn't have to wake up. I think we were having fun."

"Baby, we can have fun now. Why don't you get up and brush your teeth, then we can have room service."

"Okay. Where's my mommy?"

"I don't know, baby. Let's not worry about her for now. She's a big girl."

"Alright. I think she should be here, though."

Mila climbed out of the bed and wandered into the bathroom.

12

Chloe woke drooling, her head pounding in pain. Grace lay beside her lightly snoring. She couldn't remember much of the night before, after the first couple of Tequila shots. Still fully clothed and hot, she pulled off the lifeguard sweater she'd been wearing and stumbled into the bathroom. Her stomach was queasy, but she held it down and sat on the toilet. She shivered while she urinated and thought that she must have made a fool of herself last night. Standing to look in the mirror, she turned the water on and washed her hands and face. After rinsing her mouth, she thought to check the time. Her eyes blurred and when she gained focus she could see it was eleven thirty. Dreading her next move, she knew she should call Rebecca.

Grace began to stir in the room. She called out, "Chloe? Are you here?"

"I'm in the bathroom, sweetie."

"What the fuck happened last night? I feel like I was hit in the head with a bat."

"I hope not." Chloe walked out of the bathroom and gingerly inspected her friend. She said, "You look fine, Gracie. It's just a hangover."

Grace looked startled. She pointed and said, "Is that a spider in the corner of the wall?"

Chloe looked towards the ceiling where she was pointing. She said, "I think so!" Chloe jumped up and sprinted back to the bathroom, slamming the door and locking it. She screamed, "Kill it, Grace!"

Grace replied, "Damn, girl. I hate 'em too, but you didn't have to abandon me to die out here."

"Just kill it, Grace. I'm not coming out until you do!"

"I'll call someone."

Grace called the front desk and they said they'd send someone shortly. Hanging up the phone she laughed. Chloe asked from behind the bathroom door, "What are you laughing about?"

"Nothing, honey. The front desk is sending someone."

After the spider debacle Chloe exited the bathroom and looked at her watch. She said, "Shit, it's almost twelve o'clock. I've got to call Becca."

Grace began biting her fingernails. She said, "I'm worried about heading back to the states. I don't know if I'm ready."

Chloe said, "The time is now, sweetie. We leave today and everything is going to be fine."

Chloe picked up the phone and dialed Rebecca's room.

13

Rebecca picked up the phone and Mila looked up from the table where she sat with Barry, eating pancakes and bacon. Mila asked, "Is it my mom?"

Rebecca asked, "Where are you, Chloe?"

"I'm on the second floor. We're coming down in a minute. We're just going to eat something really quick. I'm sorry for the way I've been acting. There was a spider or I would have called sooner."

"A spider?"

"Yes. A monster." Chloe laughed nervously.

"We'll, it's alright, baby. You get down here by one o'clock, though. We'll be ready to go. I've got everything packed. You know, I'm not feeling the love lately."

"I know. I'll make it up to you, I promise"

"Beautiful. Just get your pretty butt here on time."

"I will."

When Rebecca hung up the phone Mila was on the edge of her seat. She asked, "What did mommy say?"

"She said she was held up by a monster. Now, eat your food so you can be good and strong in case the monster follows her here."

Barry said, "I ain't afraid of no monster."

Mila rolled her eyes and giggled. She said, "You wouldn't be, boo-boo."

Barry moaned. He said, "Stop calling me that."

"Why? It never bothered you before."

"Well. It does now."

Rebecca interrupted the spat. She said, "Eat your food, kiddos. We hit the road in less than an hour."

Mila stuck her tongue out at Barry and began digging into her pancakes.

14

The door to the room opened and when Chloe entered, Mila ran to her and hugged her waist. Grace walked in behind her and Rebecca squinted. Grace said, "Well, I'm ready for a three-day road trip."

Rebecca said, "Aren't we all. All you have are two bags?"

"Yeah, I travel light."

"Interesting. So are we."

Chloe said, "Let's get in the freakin' monster truck and roll."

Grace looked startled. She asked, "Monster truck?"

Chloe said, "Yeah, wait till you see this thing. Black and pink jacked up four-by-four. It's bad ass."

Mila said, "Oh, Mommy, you swear."

Chloe laughed and rolled her eyes. She said, "Yeah, sweetie, I do. Don't you copy."

"I won't. I don't want a potty mouth."

"Good." Chloe looked at Rebecca and smirked. She asked, "You ready to do this?"

Barry said, "I'm ready. I want to drive."

Chloe flushed. The sound of Barry's voice brought back the memories of the things she had said the night before. She said, "You wish, buster."

They all began picking up what little possessions they had accumulated over their stay and headed for the valet. Rebecca walked beside Chloe on the way. She said, "Did you stay up all night drinking?"

Chloe said, "I'm not sure what I did last night."

"Well, you should have taken a shower. You smell like a brewery."

Overhearing the conversation from behind, Grace laughed. She said, "Last night was a blast and we woke up too late to both shower and eat."

Rebecca said, "Well, you should have chosen showers because you two reek."

Grace retorted, "Sorry, Mom."

Rebecca's ears heated and she had the urge to put down the bag she was carrying and fight. Visions of a spin kick to the temple of the tall and belligerent woman danced in her head. The sheer nerve of the comment infuriated her. A late comeback rose inside of her and before she could stop herself she was replying.

Rebecca said, "Funny how I'm the only one of us who doesn't have children and I'm the only one acting anything like a mom."

Chloe and Grace both stopped in their tracks. Grace said, "That's a low blow."

Rebecca replied, "The truth. Low blow? I don't think so. You both need to take a good look at yourselves."

Mila and Barry looked lost in the middle of the conflict. Rebecca glanced at Mila and the look in her eyes broke Rebecca's heart. She didn't want to upset Mila and

Barry. Letting Chloe and Grace go any farther treating her like she was a downer was not going to be permissible to Rebecca. She'd had enough. She sat her bag on the ground and took Mila's hand.

She said, "Chloe? Are you with us? We won't be ignored or taunted. If things are going to work for us, you have to be on board all the way. If you want to jump ship, now is the time. Just say it. Say you want to be a family, or you and your friend can run off and get all messed up all you want. Going through what you're going through doesn't give you the right to treat us badly. You or your friend."

Grace said, "I was just being a smart ass. I'm sorry, Rebecca."

Chloe said, "I'm with you. You don't have to snap at us, though."

Rebecca let go of Mila's hand and walked up to Chloe. She looked her in the eyes and Chloe noticed that ever so familiar curious gleam. Rebecca said, "Baby, this isn't me snapping. I need you on board if we're going to make this work. You have to understand that."

"I do. We aren't going to jump ship." She looked at Grace. She asked, "Are we, Gracie?"

Grace put her hand to her mouth and bit her fingernail. She said, "I've been a jerk, right?"

Rebecca said, "I could add a few labels, but why bother. We've got to stick together and we have to be a strong unit. I'm under my own obligation. Why abuse a friendship or relationship that you will only benefit from? Your impression the other day in the bathroom was a bad one. I won't hold it against you and I can even say that we'll do a fresh start if you can refrain from treating me like the enemy."

Grace said, "I think I can do that. I don't know why I've been acting this way. It's not how I really am."

"Beautiful. Grace, we can be friends. You have to understand that I just want what's best."

"I understand."

Chloe said, "I'm sorry I let it come to this, Rebecca. Can you forgive me?"

"Baby, I already have."

Chloe embraced Rebecca. She said, "I love you."

Rebecca said, "I love you, too."

Mila's voice meek and soft interrupted them. She said, "What about me and Barry, Mommy?"

Chloe went to Mila and embraced her. She said, "Of course I love you, sweetie. I've just been going through so much in my own head. I'm sorry I've been neglecting you."

Barry said, "You don't have to say you love me, Momma. I know Poppa was my fault."

"I do love you, Barry. It's not that. I'm just so mad."

Rebecca said, "Well. How about hitting the road? We've got a few days to work everything out."

Chloe said, "I'm ready. What about you, Barry, Mila? You ready to get in the biggest truck you've ever been in in your lives?"

Mila beamed. She said, "I'm ready."

Barry nodded his head. He said, "I want to see it already."

Grace asked, "Can we share the drive time?"

Rebecca laughed. She said, "We can share a hotel, but only I drive Bessy."

15

Rebecca handed the valet her ticket and they all waited in anticipation. The kids and Grace had been hearing about this monster truck and now they were going to get to see it. Barry was likely the most excited of the bunch. Rebecca had told him stories about the truck, when she'd bought it, all the things she had done to it. He wanted to see it during their whole stay, but Rebecca wouldn't allow it. She wanted him to see it the day they left and here they were.

The black and pink crew cab machine came rumbling up and Barry went berserk. He said, "It really is a monster truck!"

The machine was shining and polished on its custom wheels and 33" tires. Rebecca had ordered it detailed while it was in the garage and it looked like a top of the line show truck with the sun shining off the thick clear coat of the custom paint. Grace and Mila were also in awe. It was the ultimate bad ass girl machine and no doubt visions of driving Bessy were playing in their minds. Imagining themselves driving up somewhere with crowds of people stopping to see who might be driving such a beast, hopping out and throwing their hair back in the wind while everyone stared.

Rebecca said, "Let's climb in and wear down some tread."

Mila said, "So cool, Aunt Rebecca. Will you bring me to school in this?"

Rebecca hadn't thought of Mila going to school. The thought made her a little sad. She didn't want to let the precious girl out of her sight after spending two nonstop weeks with her. She wondered how they were going to do it. It was almost certain that Barry would be homeschooled, but Mila could go back. The houses she'd been looking at were in a whole different school district on the other side of the metroplex. There was a good chance that she could have a normal school year. It was unlikely the young students at a school so far away from where they had been would know about the things that happened with Mila and her family.

Rebecca said, "Baby, we'll take Bessy sometimes, but the Lexus is nice, too. You know a truck like this isn't for driving every day."

"It's okay once and a while, right?"

"That's right, baby. Now let me help you get in."

Chloe opened the back door and Rebecca helped Mila up then Barry. Grace followed and once everyone was in, the bunch rumbled out the drive and on their journey. Grace said, "So much wood and ostrich leather in here. This thing must have cost a ton."

Rebecca said, "Baby, you have no idea." She turned up the radio and the bass kicked in. It was official, the adventure had begun.

16

Everyone in the backseat had dozed off and only Chloe and Rebecca remained alert. The radio was down low and the rumble of the big motor and whine of the large knobby tires were the predominant sounds. Rebecca yawned and looked over at Chloe. She smiled and thought what a beautiful creature her friend was.

Rebecca asked, "Are you tired?"

Chloe said, "I am, but I don't want you to be the only one awake."

"We'll stop at the next hotel."

Rebecca programmed the in-dash GPS to direct them to the nearest lodging. There was one forty-seven miles from their location. Rebecca grinned at Chloe. Chloe rolled her eyes. She said, "So far away."

Rebecca laughed. She said, "It's nothing, baby. We can keep each other up another thirty minutes."

"Thirty minutes?"

Rebecca stepped on the gas and the engine roared. Chloe said, "Oh my God, you're so bad."

"Baby, I was born this way."

"I've been wanting to talk to you."

"About what?"

"Us."

"What about us, baby?"

"Well. I know you like women. I don't want to be in a relationship with another man."

"Baby, let's not do this with the kids in the back seat. One of those rascals could be playing possum."

"You're right, Becca. We'll talk about it later."

"How about we talk about houses? I found some nice ones for the 'low low' in Fort Worth. Good areas. Good schools. What do you think?"

"I like Fort Worth. Do you think we can get one big enough for Grace and Darla to stay with us? I mean, if she wants. She's really not a bad person, Becca."

"I was hoping it would be just me and you, baby."

"I know. She needs us, though."

"Us?"

"Yes. You and me. She needs us in her life."

"She doesn't have to live with us for us to be in her life."

"I know. I want her to. It would be really cool, Becca."

"You know, I don't want to be around a junky. If she's going to be a party animal, it won't work."

"I understand. I'll talk to her."

"Don't talk to her about getting a house with us, yet. I've got to be around her for a while. If we get along in the next couple of weeks, I'll think about it."

"That's all I'm asking for now, Becca. Please, just think about it."

"You know, this is another one of those conversations we should have had without a potential audience."

"Well, crap. You come up with something to talk about."

"How about hunting?"

"Becca, spiders freak me out. I don't know if I can kill a large animal."

"You're right. I'll probably have to wait for Barry to grow up and go."

"I don't know how I feel about Barry with a gun."

"We're going to get that little heathen straight, baby."

Both women enjoyed a light-hearted laugh due to the comment.

17

As the hotel came into view, Chloe and Rebecca looked at each other. Chloe said, "It looks like a dump."

"Yeah, baby. We stayed in some worse dumps than this on our way here. Do you want to get two rooms?"

"I think we should."

A small voice from the back seat startled them. Barry said, "I want to sleep with you, Aunt Becca."

Rebecca looked at Chloe and raised her eyebrows. Chloe covered her mouth. There was no way to know how much conversation he had heard without asking. They pulled up at the motel and Rebecca turned in her seat. She asked Barry, "How long have you been awake?"

"I don't know. I think I just woke up."

Chloe asked, "Did you hear us talking?"

"That's what woke me up, I think."

Chloe cringed. She asked, "What were we saying?"

"Something about a dump."

Chloe breathed and sighed relief. She said, "We are at a 'dump' and we'll be here a couple of hours. Mommy has to shower and aunt Rebecca needs rest."

Rebecca said, "I'll go inside and get the rooms. Sit tight."

She hopped out of the truck and headed inside. Chloe looked around at what she could see of the property from her position in the cab of the truck. The place was painted a not so attractive avocado green that was peeling off the walls, with dark brown trim. The darkest places on the lot, where the lights were out, having been busted out, or simply not replaced by maintenance, gave the place an even more eerie feeling than what her first impression was. She didn't know if her mind was playing tricks due to boredom and sleep deprivation, but it looked like there were people lurking in the inky, black, unlit recesses of the property.

There wasn't any vehicle there that was even remotely similar to the truck they were driving in any of the occupied spaces. That wasn't unusual. Chloe hadn't seen another truck like the one they were driving, ever. The cars and trucks that were there were old and didn't look well maintained. She wondered if half of the five she could see were even operable. The scene made her uncomfortable and she wasn't sure that this eye-sore was a good place to stay the night—although it would be daylight in a few hours—the motel gave her a bad vibe.

Rebecca climbed back into the truck. She jingled two keys in front of Chloe. She said, "Got 'em. Side by side, baby."

"I don't know about this place, Becca. Really. Look at it."

"Let's ask Barry." Rebecca turned in her seat. She asked, "Barry? Are you scared of monsters?"

Barry said, "I ain't scared of no dang monster."

Rebecca smirked at Chloe. She raised her eyebrow and Chloe chuckled. Rebecca said, "I guess it's settled."

Rebecca put the truck in drive and rumbled into the parking space closest to their rooms. Chloe said, "Great, they had to give us the rooms in the darkest part of the whole place. Maybe you should go ask for some other rooms where it's lit. I don't like this."

Rebecca said, "Baby, I'm so tired. Do you really want me to go back in there?"

"I could do it."

"You don't speak Spanish, baby. Let's just get in the rooms and make it through the night."

"Okay. It better not be crawling with spiders or I'm sleeping in the truck."

"Oh, baby. You and your silly monsters."

Barry said, "Can we quit the talk and go inside? I have to pee."

Rebecca looked at Chloe and smirked. She said, "Looks like it's settled again."

Chloe groaned. She said, "Another adventure. Right?"

"That's right, baby. Let's wake everyone up and get inside. I'll share a room with Grace."

"You're going to leave me all alone?"

"You'll have the kids. Barry's not afraid of monsters. Remember?"

Barry said, "I'll protect you, Momma."

Chloe turned to wake up Grace and Mila.

18

The inside of the room was as depressing as the exterior of the building. The only lights that worked were a bedside lamp and the bathroom light. Chloe thought it was just as well. The room probably wouldn't look much better lit anyway. The two beds didn't look comfortable, like they were lumped up and covered in rags. Mila climbed in one and curled up without a peep. It amused Chloe that the young girl didn't care to complain about the accommodations after being spoiled the past few weeks at a five-star resort.

Barry said, "I'm not really tired now, Momma. Can I watch T.V.?"

Chloe went to the old turn-knob television and turned the power. It hissed and a faint glow began to show, then all at once the picture popped up and the volume kicked in loudly. The person who'd been watching it before them must have been nearly deaf. Mila sat up in the bed as Chloe turned the sound down. With a grimace on her face, Mila shook her head.

Mila said, "What the heck?"

Chloe said, "Don't worry, sweetie. Go back to bed."

Mila threw herself back into the mattress and Chloe

looked at Barry and frowned. She tried turning the channel and could only find static until the set landed right back on the Spanish soap opera it had begun on. She said, "Looks like this is it. Do you want to turn it off?"

Barry shook his head. He said, "I'll watch this."

"Okay. Mommy's going to take a shower. Don't destroy the place while I'm in there."

"I won't." Barry sat on the end of the bed. He said, "Not much to destroy. Is there?"

Chloe laughed. She said, "You're right about that."

The bathroom was dimly lit, and the bottom of the shower curtain was mildewed. The shower head had green and oxidized, white-speckled, crusty buildup on the chrome fixture. Chloe shuddered. It wasn't her first time in a dump. It might not be her last either, but she never liked ill-kept places like this one. There were things immensely creepy about this place that she didn't care for. It gave the vibe that anything might happen. From getting robbed to bed bugs and lice, these places put Chloe on alert.

The shower sputtered on in the cramped space and Chloe was reluctant to put her towel over the shower rod. She didn't want to touch the curtain and was going to have to brave the rusted and ringed tub. The water sprayed in a steady but weak stream after a couple of seconds and it was taking its sweet time warming up. She cleaned the dirt off the top of the toilet with some toilet paper and placed her towel and clothes there.

Naked and still no hot water, she decided it was time

to get it over with. When she stepped into the tub, she found what looked like the cleanest spot on the curtain and pulled it shut. The water sent chills through her and before long she had semi-adapted to the temperature. She let her hair soak and wondered what was going on in the next room. It wasn't hard to imagine an all-out brawl, but she hoped that Rebecca and Grace would get along fine.

19

Grace didn't waste any time getting comfortable. Neither she nor Rebecca were as squeamish about the run-down accommodations as Chloe. Both women were stripped down to their panties and Rebecca laid on top of the covers reading a parenting book while Grace stood in front of the mirror drying her hair.

Grace said, "I'm not gay, but you have a bangin' body."

Rebecca didn't bother looking up from her book. She asked, "Are you looking at me in the mirror?"

"A little."

"Can you see this?"

"Hey! You don't have to flip me off. I'm just saying. If I was gay, I'd want to do you."

Rebecca laughed. She put her book down, thoroughly amused. She asked, "How do you know you're not gay?"

"I don't know. I've experimented. That's about it, though. I like men."

"Well, I like both. Do you want to experiment?"

"Chloe would be pissed."

"I know. I wouldn't do it. I'm just teasing you."

"Do you two…you know."

"That's private. Why don't you ask her?"

"I don't know."

"Well. Would it matter?"

"I guess not."

"Beautiful. Now, unless you're going to get over here and give me head, I'm going to read my book."

Grace threw her towel across the room, missing Rebecca by a foot. She said, "You're so bad! I see why Chloe likes you so much." She giggled and grinned. She said, "I think we're going to get along just fine."

"Interesting. If you keep throwing things at me I doubt it."

"I get excited."

"Another interesting fact."

The trucks alarm chirped and went off. It screamed throughout the room, penetrating the thin walls like a tornado siren placed beside the window. Rebecca sprung from the bed. Grace looked like a deer caught in headlights.

20

Grace said, "Don't go out there, Rebecca."

It was too late to discourage her; she was twisting the door knob and ready for a fight. Adrenaline pumped through Rebecca's veins and when she stepped out she was confronted by two men. The small woman in lingerie didn't turn back. Aggravated and hoping her bold move would deter the thieves. She positioned herself for action.

Grace grabbed Rebecca's arm as Chloe poked her head out of the room next door. Rebecca said in Spanish to the thieves, "What the fuck do you bitches think you doing?"

The men laughed and pointed at her. She said, "You better leave or I'll fuck you up!"

One of the men pulled out a knife and started walking towards her. Grace pulled Rebecca's arm and said, "Come inside."

When the man was in striking distance he swung. Rebecca moved swiftly, twisting his arm and in a fluid motion delivering a blow to his Adams apple that made Grace's stomach turn. Chloe shrieked as the man fell to the ground making the kind of noises a cat would make choking up a hairball. The other man ran towards Rebecca and she kicked him in the solar plexus, dropping him to the ground into the parking lot gasping for air.

She spoke to them in Spanish again. She said, "Get up and die somewhere else. Or I could kill you now. It doesn't matter to me." She kicked the man's knife away and the two thieves literally started to crawl away.

Rebecca said to Chloe and Grace, "You two get ready. We're not staying here. We don't need those assholes coming back for revenge because they were taken by a woman. I'd risk it alone, but not with the kids and not without fire power."

21

The truck was silent aside from the rumble of the motor, mufflers and knobby tires singing their own tune. No one had said a word since Rebecca told them to pack their things. It was becoming an uncomfortable ride. Dawn was approaching and the next hotel that actually had some stars showed to be over one hundred miles away.

Rebecca said, "Someone could say something or we can listen to my MP3, whatever."

Mila said, "I saw you in the window, Aunt Rebecca."

Barry said, "Me, too. It was pretty cool."

Rebecca asked, "Ladies?"

Chloe squirmed in her seat. She said, "I knew you were a bad ass, but I had no idea."

Mila said, "Ohhh, Mommy. You cussed."

Chloe turned in her seat and bit her lip. She released a small giggle. She said, "Sweetie, adults can do that some. It's okay."

Mila asked, "Is it okay if I do? Because I thought it was bad ass, too."

Chloe gasped. She said, "Young lady, don't start with the nonsense."

Barry said, "I know all kinds of cuss words. Some I don't even know what they mean. Like when we were with grandpa and grandma and grandpa was spanking Mila he called her a cunt. What does that mean?"

Grace said, "Bubba, we're not about to start explaining curse words to you two. Now simmer down before your mother blows a gasket."

Chloe was in shock and infuriated: More about the fact that while beating her daughter, Martin Apple was yelling disgusting profanities at the poor girl, than the prospect of Barry repeating them.

Mila said, "Let's not talk no more. Let's listen to the MP3."

Grace said "We ought to drive to his house now and take turns messing him up."

Rebecca said, "No need. We won't be dealing with him again."

She turned on the in-dash and turned up rap music. Chloe rolled her eyes. More swear words for the heathens. Rebecca's music was far from the clean version and that's what the peculiar woman liked to drive to the most. Goose bumps rose on Chloe's arms when the thought of what happened to Puffs Bakery just because they made Chloe cry. It wasn't hard to believe that someone who would rob and burn an establishment to the ground so quickly might not have some diabolical scheme brewing for the people who abused the children whom she had no doubt come to love.

She was brought out of her thoughts by Rebecca. Rebecca said, "Damn, I'm getting pulled over."

All heads turned to the back of the vehicle except Barry's. Rebecca said, "Calm down, people. That's not proper procedure. Eyes front."

Everyone turned around to face the front. Rebecca said, "I'll do all the talking. Hopefully this guy isn't a jerk."

Rebecca pulled to the side as the police car approached. When the officer got out of his vehicle and came to the door he was too short to see inside, though, he was not a short man. He said in Spanish, "Step out of the vehicle, ma'am."

Rebecca climbed out of the vehicle and he laughed. He said, "Is there a man with you?"

Rebecca said, "No. Just a small boy and women."

He laughed hysterically and Rebecca thought he must be going mad. He said, "I had to see for myself. Two men reported an American in a large truck beat them up and robbed them. Some people saw them suffering from a beating and I was called. The night manager of the business said a woman was driving the large truck."

"Yes. Two men tried to break into my truck and when I confronted them there was a fight. I can assure you I have no need to rob anyone."

"I see. Well. I could take you in for assault."

"I was the victim."

"I hear what you are saying."

"What does the ticket cost?"

"Well. You could pay it now. If you have one hundred dollars American."

"That's fine."

Rebecca reached in her pocket and pulled out two one hundred dollar bills."

She said, "Take them both in case I need to assault anyone else in your territory."

He took the money and smiled showcasing one lonely gold tooth right in the front and crooked yellow companions. He said, "Have a nice passage, ma'am."

"Oh, I'm sure I will."

22

Rebecca climbed back into the truck and everyone stayed silent. Curious tension filled the cab of the vehicle and no one so much as shifted in their seat. Rebecca wanted to laugh, and the only thing that stopped her from breaking into a hysterical fit was that she derived pleasure from the building curiosity of the group that she could taste in the air like a fine wine. They traveled up the ill-paved road for a couple hundred yards until Grace spoke up.

She asked, "Did you beat up the cop?"

Everyone started laughing except Rebecca. She said, "It was a scam."

Chloe asked, "What do you mean?"

"He just wanted money."

"He pulled you over to get money?"

"Yeah. He had an excuse, baby, but I knew it was a scam as soon as he started talking."

"What did he say?"

"It doesn't matter. I paid him, but hopefully we don't have to pay our way across Mexico. We've got a long way to go. You already know. It took us over three days to get to Cancun. I don't know how we made it without trouble,

I was kind of expecting it. Anyway, that place is behind us and we'll alternate driving and sleeping this time." Rebecca smirked to herself, lavishing in the adrenaline rush-inducing adventure that their trip home was becoming.

Grace said, "I thought only you drove Bessy."

"Baby, every now and then I make exceptions."

Grace said, "I can drive. I slept a long time before we stopped and I'm not tired at all."

Rebecca pulled the truck to the side of the road with a sigh. She said, "I'm drained. My adrenaline is running low and I think I've had enough, for now."

Chloe said, "We won't wreck your truck, Becca." In a playful tone.

"Baby, at this point I don't give a damn."

23

Everyone was asleep except Grace. She'd been driving for hours and the road she was on teetered the truck side to side. It was early afternoon and her eyes felt strained from concentrating on the road. A man came into view, in the middle of the narrow dirt path. A large cart blocked the road completely and he looked like he may be in distress.

Grace slowed to a halt a few yards away from the disheveled looking roadblock. The man looked like he was wearing rags and the cart had nothing in it but dirt and a thin layer of hay. He waved his arms and came around to the side of the truck. He was saying something in Spanish. Grace didn't roll down the window, but instead turned to the passenger seat where Rebecca was leaning back sleeping.

She shook Rebecca and when her eyes opened, Grace said, "There's a man out here and I don't speak Spanish."

She turned back to look at the man, he'd climbed up on the truck and she hadn't noticed. He was holding a pistol, pointing it at her. Startled she pressed the gas and the truck roared forward. The man shot the window just before the loud and jarring collision with the buggy in the road; it knocked him off the truck's step. Rebecca sat up quickly. Everyone in the truck was awake and bewildered.

Rebecca asked, "What the fuck just happened?"

Grace felt panicky.—the thought of almost being shot shook her to her bone marrow. She said, "I was trying to tell you. There was some guy."

Chloe asked, "Was that a gunshot? Did you run him over? What did you hit?"

"I don't know if I ran him over. I hit his buggy and he fell off the side of the truck. I hope the asshole is dead."

"So, it was a gunshot?"

Rebecca said, "Yes, baby, look at the window."

Chloe said, "It looks like he threw a rock."

"Baby, it's bullet proof glass. I had the truck armored when I bought it. It better work good too, that treatment costs a small fortune. Now, Grace. Slow down, baby. You're going way too fast. That leech-face bozo is far behind us now. No threat."

Grace let off the gas and pulled to the side of the road. She looked at her trembling hands and a tear escaped her eye. She said, "I think it's someone else's turn to drive."

Mila said, "I'm scared."

Barry said, "I'll protect you, sissy."

"Hey you can't call me sissy if I can't call you boo-boo."

"It's okay, sissy. You can call me that. I don't care."

Mila hugged Barry. Rebecca said, "I've had enough

sleep. I'll drive."

Chloe said, "I should argue for my turn, right?"

Rebecca said, "It's okay, baby. I got this."

24

They alternated several more times in order to make the non-stop trip, and when the border checkpoint came into view, the children cheered and the ladies were relieved. Without incident, they made it through the checkpoint and only had a short trip ahead of them, comparatively speaking.

The trip through Texas to Rebecca's apartment was uneventful—unless you count *someone's* silent assault on everyone's nostrils, a villain who never admitted or sought to be excused for their foul deed. It was Chloe's suspicion that the gas bombs were Barry's doing, but what was she supposed to do? After all, they were silent and although it was his M.O., she simply had no proof. Whoever the culprit was, they may take the disgusting secret to their grave. Maybe the deviant even derived pleasure from the sneaky torture, or had been just too embarrassed to confess to the nauseous volley. It was an odor like a busted sewerage line on a hot summer day. The kind of thing that immediately conjured mental pictures of the giant turd it must be seeping its way around.

They all exited the vehicle in the apartment parking

lot except for Rebecca, who had the honor of parking the enormous, recently-soiled truck in the garage, windows down. Everyone looked at each other in suspicion, except Barry, who seemed to care less. Chloe thought, every dog likes his own brand. She shook her head and scrunched her nose. Mila looked green in the face. She also believed it was him. As stated before, no proof. All the same.

Chloe said, "Whoever that was in the truck is horrible. Barry. Are you sure it wasn't you? You little stinker."

Barry shook his head. He said, "I dinnit do it."

Chloe looked at Grace and smirked. She said, "What do you think about that, Gracie?"

"I don't know what to think."

"Yeah, me either."

Rebecca emerged from the garage. She said, "I'm going in the apartment and I'm not coming out for a week."

The group made their way to the apartment with bags in hand. Grace asked, "How many bedrooms do you have?"

"I've got two bedrooms and an office. The office has a pull-out couch. That's where you'll stay."

Rebecca unlocked the door and stepped aside. Barry and Mila were the first ones over the threshold. Mila said, "Whoa. This place is nice, Aunt Rebecca. Is that rug a real bear?"

Rebecca passed through the doorway and went straight for the kitchen. She said, "Yes, Mila. I killed him. Look around the rest of the house, baby."

Mila asked, "Can I sleep on the bear?"

Rebecca popped open a bottle of wine. She said, "Ladies? A celebration? Yes, Mila. If it's okay with your mommy you can sleep on that bear all you want."

Mila said, "Mommy, please." Showing her best 'have pity' expression.

Chloe said, "It's fine with me, sweetie. Go get cleaned up. You, too, Barry. I'll make you something to eat in a minute." Chloe accepted a glass from Rebecca and Grace followed suit.

Rebecca raised her glass, and said, "We're here. To survival."

Grace said, "Amen to that."

They swigged from their glasses and Barry came into the kitchen where they were standing. He said, "Everything is black and white."

Rebecca said, "It most certainly is, baby."

Grace looked over the furniture herself and thought it was all in good taste. She had the same kinds of curiosities about Rebecca as Chloe had when she first stepped foot in the residence. Who was this extraordinary creature? Such thoughts Rebecca Frost conjured in all who made her acquaintance.

Barry asked, "Mommy, can I sleep with you?"

She wanted to tell him that he had to sleep on the couch. Spending the night being gassed after the long ride wasn't appealing. She wondered if he wanted to sleep with her so that he could exact that sort of torture on her. But she figured he'd probably expelled the culprit turd already. It must have been plopped into the toilet when he was in the bathroom. What a little sneak, she thought.

Chloe said, "I guess. As long as you don't steal the covers."

Rebecca finished her glass of wine. She said, "I'm toasted. Time to shower and sleep. I'll see you all tomorrow afternoon." She laughed. A short and pleasant sound that eased the room.

Grace said, "I'm going to shower in the guest bathroom first, if that's okay, Chloe?"

Rebecca walked out from the back one more time with a comforter and pillow for Mila. She kissed the young girl's forehead and without another word, retreated to her room. Grace made haste to the bathroom and left Chloe staring down at Barry. Chloe didn't want to hate her son. Her impulse was to hug him. Barry didn't like affection much, so she let the feeling pass.

She asked, "Do you want something to eat or drink?"

Mila walked up. She said, "I do."

"Okay. I'll make you two something. After we eat and your aunt Gracie is out of the bathroom it's shower time. Starting with one of you."

Mila looked at Barry. She said, "You should go first, boo-boo. You're the smelliest."

Barry shrugged his shoulders. He said, "I don't care."

Mila said, "I know you don't. That was bad in the truck. How could you do that to us?"

"I dinnit do it."

"I know it was you." Mila screwed her face into a

grimace and Chloe could see she was frustrated.

Chloe said, "That's enough. Just drop it, and I don't want to hear about it again."

Mila climbed on to one of the kitchen island stools. She said, "I'm glad we're here. That trip was crazy."

"It sure was, sweetie."

Chloe turned and began preparing the food.

25

The warm water felt relaxing to Chloe. She let it run through her hair and down her back trying not to think of anything at all. Her thoughts kept wandering to Peter, despite her efforts not to think. Days when he would come home from work and they'd take showers together. That fateful day he was shot and his blood that covered her face. Knowing that she would never take another shower with him or feel his touch and the feel of his hand in hers made Chloe weak in the knees. She had to sit in the tub and she let the tears flow freely for the first time in days. She sobbed and spoke quietly.

She said, "I'm so sorry, Peter. I know I should be strong, but I don't know how I'm going to do this. How am I supposed to make it through this life without you? I feel weak. Why? I don't understand. I just want you back." Chloe sobbed.

26

When she exited the bathroom, Chloe noticed a light emanating from under the office door. Grace was either awake or she was sleeping with the lights on. Chloe walked up and listened, there were no sounds coming from inside. She tapped on the door lightly with her fingernail. No response. About to leave, her curiosity got the best of her. She twisted the knob to find it was unlocked. She slowly opened the door and peeked inside.

Grace covered herself quickly. She asked, "What are you doing, Chloe?"

Chloe said, "I'm sorry, I thought you were sleeping. I was just checking on you."

"Well, I'm not sleeping. I was listening to an audiobook on my headphones."

Chloe emitted a nervous laugh. She said, "It must be a good one. I'll leave you alone." She began to close the door.

Grace said, "Hold on. You can stay. If you want."

"I don't know, Grace. You looked occupied."

"Oh, shut up and get in here. Don't act like you've never masturbated before. I forgot to lock the stupid door."

Chloe entered the room and sat on the edge of the bed. Grace said, "You look like something's bothering you. What's wrong?"

"I can't stop thinking of Peter. All the things he will miss out on, and how much I miss him. I'm a nervous wreck and now that little heathen Barry is in my bed. What am I going to do? I can't get the day Peter was shot out of my mind. I see it over and over. Every time I look at Barry I get angry inside. I know it's horrible. I'm trying to forgive him for what he did to make this happen, but it's so hard. I just wanted to throw him out of the window of the truck today. The stench was horrible and he refused to admit it or take a poop at the last stop. I want to be a good person, a good mom. I feel chaotic inside. Like I'm going to lose it and do something crazy."

"I'm so embarrassed, Chloe."

"Don't be. I've masturbated a lot. I've never admitted it to anyone except Peter, but I'm kind of a compulsive masturbator. I know it's strange for a woman, I guess. I've never talked to anyone about it, like I said. I haven't done it since Peter died, though. I just feel so sad."

"Oh, well, that's...interesting. I was saying I'm embarrassed about something else."

Chloe's cheeks reddened. She said, "Oh my God. I just outed myself for no reason."

"It's okay, honey. Not like I'll go tellin' the world."

"What are you so embarrassed about, Gracie?"

Grace started biting her fingernail and the thought of where the finger had been flashed in Chloe's mind. She shook her head. She said, "You can tell me. I won't tell anyone."

"Really? It's bad."

"I promise."

"I was the one in the truck."

Chloe gasped. She asked, "Are you serious?"

Grace said, "It was that place we ate at in Mexico, I think. It gave me the worst gas."

"That is malevolent, Grace. I could freakin' taste it."

The embarrassed look on Grace's face cooled Chloe's frustration. Grace said, "There was nothing I could do, Chloe. I couldn't hold them in."

"You don't have to tell me, I know. You could have killed us." Chloe laughed.

Grace said, "You promised. You're not going to tell anyone, right?"

"I thought it was sexual or something. I don't know about this. I might have to spill the beans." She nudged Grace on the leg. "Get it?"

Grace pleaded. She said, "Chloe, please. I don't want Rebecca and the kids to know. I'll fall over dead with embarrassment."

Chloe rolled her eyes. She said, "Alright, I won't tell. You know you're going to owe me."

"I do have the compulsive masturbation thing."

Chloe giggled. She said, "Yeah, I guess you have that on me. We'll just call it a tie for now."

27

Morning peeked brightly through the curtains in Chloe's room as she opened her eyes and smelled coffee brewing. She wondered who was up so early. She crawled out of bed, careful not to wake Barry. Stealthily she made her way out of the room and down the hallway. Rebecca was sitting at the kitchen island reading a newspaper and sipping from a mug inscribed 'Bad Bitch'.

Chloe walked up and without looking up from her paper, Rebecca said in a low and seductive tone, "There's more in the pot, baby."

Chloe made herself a cup and sat next to her peculiar friend. She said, "I thought you weren't getting up for days, Becca."

"I lied. It's Monday morning. I have things I want to do."

"Like what?"

"I want to go look at a house in Fort Worth, and I need to go by our lawyer's office sometime today. Now that you're awake you can go with me, if you want. He has papers for both of us to sign to finalize the adoption."

"Are you sure you still want to adopt them? Even after

the way I acted in Cancun?"

"It's all the more reason for me to adopt them. They need more than just you to rely on."

Chloe turned red in the face and she bit her lip. Rebecca said, "I don't mean it like that, baby. You know what I mean. Joint custody is beneficial for them in many ways and I'll be honored to call them mine. There's just one other thing. We are going to need to get married."

Chloe swallowed hard. She said, "If you're proposing, it's not very romantic."

"I think it would be best."

"My husband died less than a month ago, I can't get married so soon."

"It's not mandatory. We can talk about it later. Wait until you see this house I found. I hope the picture is accurate."

Chloe rolled her eyes. She said, "Way to change the subject, Becca."

"Baby, I know you don't want to talk about it. We can wait as long as you'd like. Go get dressed and I'll wake Grace. We'll ask her to watch the kids."

28

Chloe and Rebecca rode in silence for a while. The Lexus was a lot quieter and smoother than the big Chevy truck. Sitting in the car, watching trees and homes pass by, Chloe's mind worked manically. She wanted to get the nerve to have the conversation that plagued her thoughts. Being married wasn't something she could consider so soon after Peter's death.

Rebecca said, "You can turn on the radio."

"Becca, that's the third time you've said that since we left the apartment. I don't want the radio. I want you to say what's on your mind."

"I'd like you to say what's on your mind. I don't know what you mean. I think I say everything I have to say."

Chloe rolled her eyes. She said, "You know what's on my mind. How could you suggest we get married? It hasn't been long enough and we haven't been together. I don't even know if I'll like it. I've never been with a woman."

"Baby, it's not about sex."

"Well, if I'm going to marry someone it certainly has something to do with sex and attraction."

Rebecca smirked and raised an eyebrow. She asked,

"Aren't you attracted to me?"

Chloe giggled then bit her lip. She said, "Don't start that Rebecca. You know you're attractive to pretty much anyone who lays their eyes on you. "

"Baby, you're being too kind. Besides, I'm not for everybody."

Chloe began fidgeting and bit her lip. Rebecca asked, "Why do you seem nervous?"

"I don't want to lose you, Becca. It's just too soon. You have to understand."

"I do, baby. I anticipated your answer. I still wanted you to know what was on my mind so I put it out there. It's not a rush and you won't lose me, I'm yours."

They pulled up in front of a large Victorian style, modern home with a circular driveway and well-manicured lawn. Everything was trimmed from the bushes to the flower garden. It was a hulking structure with sharp points and tall windows. White and blue brick and paint covered the structure; it looked like it could be a castle in a fairy tale.

Chloe gasped. She asked, "Is this the house, Becca?"

"Yes."

"It looks like a mansion. It must cost a fortune."

"I have investments and money squirreled away as you know."

"You have enough legal money to buy this?"

"Baby, I have enough legal money to buy ten of these."

29

When the day came to move, Mila was ecstatic. She said, "I can go to school here. No one knows me. The house is so big."

Grace had followed in Chloe's car. She exited and approached the group. She said, "How many rooms is this place?"

Rebecca looked at her with the curious look she gave so well. She said, "The main home is six bedrooms, five and a half baths with two living rooms, an oversized kitchen, and dining room. It also has a library and separate office. How about we go inside and look around?"

Barry said, "I like it. It looks cool."

Grace asked, "What do you mean the main house?"

Rebecca said, "Well, there's a pool out back and a two-bedroom guest house with changing stalls. I'll probably rent it out. If you're interested."

Chloe smiled wide. She said, "That would be perfect, Grace."

Grace said, "Let's check this place out before I agree to anything."

Rebecca laughed and put her hand out in a motion

that said, 'Right this way.' Everyone entered the interior of the home like a pack of students on a sightseeing tour. Chloe watched Rebecca like the tour guide and admired how easily she explained and presented every little detail of the home. It was a better presentation than they had been given by the realtor when they had come on their own. She knew that Rebecca had been into the Real Estate world for a while, and watching her friend gave her butterflies in her stomach. She figured that Rebecca must be doing very well.

Mila said, "All the windows are so big and it's like a castle. I'm gonna feel like a princess!"

Rebecca said, "You are a princess, baby."

Mila wrapped herself around Rebecca's waist and squeezed. She said, "I love you, Aunt Becca."

Grace asked, "Can we go look at the guest house?"

Chloe said, "That would be nice."

The three women went to look at the small bungalow in the back yard and let the kids have free roam of the house and property for a while. The inside of the guest house was well kept. Everything was white and yellow. Grace ran her finger across the front windowsill and said, "Wow, there isn't a speck of dust."

Rebecca said, "I had everything cleaned. Who wants to move into a dirty home?" Rebecca laughed.

Chloe said, "I think this would be a great place for you and Darla, Grace. We could see each other all the time like this."

Rebecca said, "You can stay in the main house with us if you want. I thought that maybe you'd like something of your own. The four-car garage is attached and there's an electric gate to get back here. I think you can feel safe and secure in this place and have your own space. What do you think?"

Grace wiped her tearing eyes. She said, "I'm just so happy that you're going to make me a part of your lives. I was worried y'all would ditch me."

Chloe went to Grace and embraced her. She said, "We're going to get Darla and we're going to be there for you all the way. Aren't we, Becca?"

Rebecca nodded her head. She said, "Yes, baby. We'll help her any way we can. You have us, Grace."

Barry and Mila showed up at the guest house and they were full of energy. Mila jumped up and down. She asked, "Can we go swimming?"

Rebecca said, "The movers will be here soon with all of our things. Let's wait until they leave."

Mila stopped bouncing around and frowned. She said, "Okay, Aunt Becca."

Barry said, "I'm gonna go to school here too. I wanna try."

Chloe's skin crawled. She said, "We're going to homeschool you, Barry. You remember."

"I wanna try, though, Momma."

Rebecca said, "We'll talk about it later, baby. How about we order some pizza and stuff ourselves?"

Barry and Mila spoke in unison. They exclaimed, "Yeah!"

It was nerve wracking to Chloe that Barry wanted to go back to school after all that had happened at Clinton

Elementary. She didn't want to have to deal with any unusual acts of violence in this new area and she didn't want his behavior affecting Mila. This was their new start. If he did anything to jeopardize the opportunity they had to live a normal life, again, she didn't know how she would react. It was hard enough containing herself as it was.

When the children ran for the house, Rebecca said to Chloe, "Don't worry, baby. I'll talk to him."

Grace said, "It might not be a bad idea to give him another chance at having a normal life. Mila was getting bullied at the other school. That's what started the whole thing, right?"

Chloe said, "It's more than that, Gracie. He has some issues. He doesn't play well with others."

"Lots of five-year-olds don't, honey. He could get in there and do fine."

Rebecca said, "He would do fine being homeschooled, also. I'm going to talk with him and see what he really wants. The schools around here are very prep and I plan on sending Mila to a private one. If he wanted to go it would have to be public school, which is great in this area, but I'd like to keep them at different places so that one doesn't affect the other."

Chloe rolled her eyes and huffed. She asked, "Were you going to talk to me about all of this?"

"Of course, baby. We'll talk about it tonight if you'd like, but for now, let's order some pizza."

30

Rebecca had Mila and Barry's rooms furnished and had organized them with the things from their old home in Dallas. Her room and the office along with Chloe's room had boxes everywhere. Chloe didn't want anything from the old house so all of her things were donated to a charity and her room consisted of the same furniture from the guest room of the apartment. Grace settled in to the office with the fold out couch and everything was quiet except the classical music that played throughout the residence over built-in home surround speakers.

Chloe sat at the edge of Rebecca's bed and frowned. She said, "How will I repay you?"

Rebecca said, "Please, baby. Not this again. I told you what's mine is yours and I meant it. You will never owe me anything and I'll say it as many times as you need to hear it."

Chloe said, "I want to finish the conversation we were having in the truck that night."

"What conversation, baby?"

Rebecca went to the bed and sat next to Chloe. She smoothed Chloe's long blonde hair. She said, "If you're talking about our relationship, we don't have to do that now."

"I want to. I want you to know how I feel."

"Go on."

"Well. I love you, Becca. I don't want to be with another man after Peter. I want to be with you. I just feel like I'm doing something wrong."

"It's okay to feel like that, baby. I understand. Peter meant the world to you and I know that. We can be together, and it doesn't have to be now."

Chloe said, "I want it to be now." She leaned over and kissed Rebecca.

Rebecca pulled back. Chloe asked, "What's wrong?"

"Baby, you're not ready."

"I am."

"No. I don't think you are. You need more time to grieve. Let's give it some time."

Chloe asked, "Don't you love me?" A tear escaped her eye and rolled slowly down her pale cheek.

Rebecca said, "I love you dearly. That's why we have to wait a little longer. It's important to me that you're ready before we go any further."

"Can I sleep with you tonight?"

"If you mean sex, I don't think so."

"Not sex, Becca. I just need you to hold me."

"I can do that, but don't get fresh." Rebecca smirked and winked.

Chloe bit her lip and went in for another kiss. Rebecca put her hand up. She asked, "What are you doing?"

"It's just kissing, Becca. No sex."

Rebecca raised an eyebrow and locked lips with

Chloe.

31

Rebecca woke and stared at Chloe for a minute. The beautiful woman was sound asleep and looked serene. Light peering in from the window danced around Chloe's pale features and Rebecca smiled in amazement and awe. When Chloe opened her eyes, she blinked for focus. She smiled at Rebecca. She asked, "How long have you been watching me?"

"Not long."

"That was the first night in a while I went without having a nightmare. At least one I can remember. You're good luck."

"I hope so, baby." Rebecca didn't want to tell her she heard her whimpering in the night. Not being able to remember and believing she had a peaceful night could help Chloe keep a positive attitude throughout the day.

There was a knock at the door and Mila poked her head in. She asked, "Aunt Becca? Have you seen…oh, Mommy. Why didn't y'all invite me? I like pajama parties."

Chloe sat up in the bed. She said, "I'm sorry, sweetie. Come on, get up here."

Mila climbed up and snuggled between the two

women. She said, "Your bed is comfy, Aunt Becca. Aunt Gracie is cooking pancakes. Are y'all hungry?"

Rebecca said, "I'm starving. What do you want to do today, Mila?"

"I want to swim. Can we do that??"

"Sure, baby. Let's get ready and after we eat and relax a little, we'll get in the pool. How does that sound?"

"Awesome."

Chloe smiled and bit her lip. She was happy with the way Rebecca interacted with the kids. It brought tears to her eyes and she tried not to show that it was choking her up. She climbed out of the bed and wandered towards the bedroom door. She said, "I'm getting in the shower and I'll meet you two at the breakfast table."

She left the room in a hurry and went to her room to get fresh clothes. In her room, alone, she breathed in a deep breath and exhaled slowly. Peter was gone and the life she was leading felt extraordinary, but there would always be a void. Guilt twanged deep in her stomach. It was difficult to bear what he might think of her now. She would like to believe that he would want her to do whatever it took to move on and live life without him. In the moment, she felt him beside her. She spoke out loud.

"I'm sorry, Peter."

Goosebumps covered her arms and she sank to the floor sobbing.

32

The warm sun felt good on Chloe's lotion-lathered skin, poolside, listening to the children's laughter and the sound of splashing water. It was relaxing and surreal, being in that place and time. Rebecca stretched out in the chase lounge beside her. She said, "Just think, baby. We can skinny dip when the children aren't here."

Chloe looked over and admired Rebecca's blue string bikini that barely covered the perfect tan body. She said, "You're practically skinny dipping now, Becca."

"Baby, I wish. I like being nude."

"I wish I tanned like you. I'm so pale I burn too quick."

"I like you pale, baby. You're gorgeous."

Mila screamed and drew the attention of everyone. She yelled, "There's a poop in the water!"

Grace and the children exited the pool and Chloe was livid. She blinked to clear her eyes. The children ran to the house and Rebecca followed to sort out the mayhem. Chloe looked at Grace and Grace shook her head. Chloe said, "Please tell me it wasn't you this time."

Grace laughed. She said, "No way. I think we all know who the culprit was this time. It's horrible. I'll get the net and you go talk to boo-boo as Mila calls him. He was laughing running up to the house. Can you believe the nerve?"

"Oh, I believe it."

Chloe entered the house and could hear Rebecca talking to Barry. Rebecca asked, "Why would you put a candy bar in the pool?"

Barry said, "I thought it was funny."

Chloe walked up and pulled the back of Barry's shorts out. She said, "You didn't put any candy bar in the pool, you pooped your pants. Go in the bathroom and I'll meet you in there. Right now!"

Barry scurried away. Rebecca said, "Don't be too hard on him. He's embarrassed."

"He ought to be, Becca. He took a crap in the pool."

Mila said, "Eww, I almost bumped into it."

Rebecca said, "These things happen, Chloe. Don't let your feelings for him and his past behavior make you any more sour about this than you need to be."

Chloe rolled her eyes. She said, "He's such a heathen. I can't stand it."

"He's still just a little boy, baby. I'll handle it if you want."

"No. I got it. I'm calm."

"Beautiful. Remember he does have feelings. He wouldn't have tried to cover it up if he wasn't embarrassed."

"I'll try not to rip his little head off."

Grace walked in and cocked her hip to the side. She asked Mila, "Are you thirsty, short stuff? Let's get a drink."

"Okay, Aunt Gracie. I don't want nothing to eat after that, though. It was so disgusting."

"I know, honey. Come with Aunt Grace and let's try to forget all about it." Grace winked at Chloe and left the room with Mila.

Chloe huffed and shook her head, then headed for Barry's bathroom.

33

Rebecca sat holding Barry's hand and listened to him rattle off reasons he should go to school. It wasn't a very convincing argument. It consisted mostly around him having friends. Not that Rebecca didn't believe he could make friends. He may make plenty of friends, then again, he might not, and then how would he react? There was also the question, did he want friends at all?

Rebecca said, "Friends won't keep you out of trouble, baby. If you stay with me, we get to spend the whole day together and I get to teach you things. Don't you want to spend the day with me and your mother?"

"I do, but I wanna go to school, too. I won't be bad."

"You keep saying that, but I don't know if I believe you. I'm going to have to talk with your mommy some more and we'll make a decision."

Barry furrowed his brow displeased with Rebecca's reply. She felt amused by his reaction and rustled his hair. Barry said, "You just want to keep me in the house all to yourself."

Rebecca laughed. She asked, "Is that such a bad thing? I just want what's best for you."

"I already know what my momma is gonna say. She

doesn't want me goin' to school either."

"We just don't want you in trouble that can be avoided. Whatever we decide it's for your best interest. Do you believe me?"

"I believe you."

"Beautiful."

34

Rebecca knocked lightly on Chloe's door. When Chloe asked her in, Rebecca sat in a chair in front of the vanity mirror. She smirked and watched Chloe get ready for bed. Her talks with Mila and Barry went well and she needed Chloe's opinion. The adoption papers had gone through and actually having a say as a parent made her feel good.

Rebecca said, "I think we should enroll Mila in the private school tomorrow and that Barry needs to be homeschooled until he gets a little older. He wants to go, but I don't think he's ready."

Chloe shook her head. She said, "He may never be ready. He's so bad."

"He's been being pretty good lately. Besides, he can't help it. I think we should keep him home this year and discuss next year over summer."

"That sounds good to me, but I don't have as much faith as you do. He'll do something crazy before long. It never fails."

"He's going to be just fine with us. You'll see."

Chloe rolled her eyes. She said, "I don't know why you think you can change him."

"Everyone's capable of change, especially with guidance and direction, baby. Give me a chance and Barry *will* be going in the right direction before you know it."

"I hope you're right. I can't deal with much more of his bullshit."

Rebecca said, "He's just a baby, Chloe. You do realize that, right?"

"He's young, but he's no baby. Barry has the soul of an accomplished deviant."

"Beautiful. We'll get along fine then."

Chloe laughed. She said, "I bet you will."

"Do you want me to sleep with you tonight?"

"No. I don't want the kids to get the wrong idea."

"Would it be wrong, baby?"

"Right now, it would be. Remember, we're taking it slow, right?"

"You're right. Baby, we can take it as slow as you want. I'm not going anywhere."

35

Mila was excited to be going to an all-girl private school. She missed going to school and interacting with other girls her own age. When they pulled up in the circle drive to drop her off Mila looked out of the window at all the other girls in their uniforms and she loved it. She loved her uniform and she loved Rebecca for getting her in this place.

Rebecca said, "I remember my first day here. It was exciting. Are you excited, baby?"

"I am, Aunt Rebecca. Thank you for bringing me here."

Mila leaned across the console and hugged Rebecca. She said, "I love you, Aunt Becca."

Rebecca hugged her back and felt a swell of pride for the girl. She said, "I'll be waiting right here when you get out and you can tell me all about your day. You go make lots of friends, baby. I love you so much."

Mila exited the car and turned to give one more wave before mingling with the crowd. Rebecca adored the way Mila looked in her little uniform and she felt nervous hoping that Mila would have a good day. She smiled as she mused how good it felt to be a mother. Barry was waiting at home with Chloe, and Rebecca knew it would be an interesting day with him. She thought to herself that taking care of the children was a feeling she would not grow tired of any time soon.

36

Chloe and Grace sat at the kitchen island and ate cereal. Grace said, "Rebecca said I didn't have to start paying rent for the guest house until I found a job. I've gotta become a real person again soon. Don't I?"

Chloe rolled her eyes and then smirked. She said, "You've been running for so long from that abusive asshole Kevin that you've forgotten how to live a normal life. He can't touch you with us, Grace. We'll protect you."

"I hope you're right about that. He's a real jerk and I don't think he will give Darla up easily."

"Becca has lawyers, Gracie, and you already saw how she handled those guys in Mexico. If he comes around here looking for trouble she might even shoot him."

"It's not good enough, Chloe. I can't rely on Rebecca to protect me. I've gotta learn how to defend myself. Do you think she will teach me?"

"We can ask her. I'd like to learn some of that stuff, too. Let's ask her when she gets home."

Chloe perked up when she heard the front door open. She said, "Let me talk to her first."

She stood and headed for the front door. A strange

girl's voice called out, "Hello."

Chloe froze in her tracks and looked back at Grace. Grace shrugged her shoulders. Chloe went to the foyer and found a pale brunette girl in a black and white uniform. She looked nervous and had a suitcase on the floor sitting next to her. Chloe thought she couldn't be much older than nineteen.

The girl said, "I was sent here by Mrs. Rebecca. She gave me a key." The girl held the key up for Chloe to see. She said, "I hope I didn't startle you. Maybe I should have rung the bell? I'm so sorry. I was hired yesterday through the service. I go to college and this is so I can make it. I pay my own way. I really appreciate this opportunity. I'm good with kids. I have four siblings and I took care of them and cleaned the house and cooked. I'm sorry if I talk too much. I do that when I get nervous. I won't do it all the time, I promise."

Chloe put her hand up halting the girls never ending speech. She called out to Grace. She said, "Grace! Come meet..."

"Noma Rae." The girl's embarrassment wasn't well concealed.

"Come meet Noma Rae, Grace!"

Grace popped around the corner smiling and dwarfing the short girl. She asked, "And what is Noma Rae doing here, Chloe?"

Chloe said, "I'm not exactly sure. Are you going to stay here, Noma?"

"Oh, yes ma'am. I'm going to help with the cooking and cleaning and children. Anything you need. I'm a good worker. I'm not the lazy type at all. I get up early in the morning. I can take the kids to school, pick them up. Anything you need. I have two younger brothers and two younger sisters, so I'm good with boys and girls. I'll be a help. It doesn't matter what room you put me in. I could stay in the basement on a cot. My family is poor and I slept on the couch anyway. I'm going to college so I can have a better life and help support my family. I'm sorry. I'm doing it again."

Grace said, "You sure can talk fast. What's with the uniform?"

"Oh, the agency gave it to me. They gave me three. They said I need to be professional. I don't mind wearing it. It's not like I get hung up on looks. People say I'm pretty, but I think I'm average. You know I—"

Chloe said, "Please, Noma. Slow down. You won't have to stay in the basement and I'm positive you don't have to wear that uniform unless you absolutely want to. We have a room available and I'm sure that's the one Rebecca wants you to have. You'll have your own bathroom and everything."

"Wow, I've never had my own bathroom. Me and my brothers and sisters had to share everything. The mornings were the worst. I met Rebecca when she gave me the key to the house. She seems real nice."

Chloe and Grace smiled at each other. Chloe said, "Come with me and I'll show you the room."

Chloe showed Noma her room and the girl lost it. Noma went inside and started opening every drawer to the huge oak dresser and flung herself on the plush unused bed. She stood and started dancing around giggling. Chloe was amused, but had to wonder where the young student got all the energy.

Chloe asked, "Do you do drugs?"

"Oh, no. No thank you. I'd never touch the stuff. When my daddy left, my momma said that he was on drugs. She said he treated her real bad and before he started messing with all that junk he was the sweetest guy. I'm not judging you, really, I'm not. I just don't use drugs. They'll mess your life up. Not that your life is messed up. You look healthy and you seem nice."

Chloe laughed. She said, "I'm not on drugs. I was just asking because you have so much energy."

Noma giggled and twirled her hair around her finger. She said, "I'm sorry. I have a lot of energy. It's just the way I am. I hope it doesn't bother you too much. I've got music in my head and I like to dance to it."

Chloe said, "It doesn't bother me, sweetie."

"Oh, great. I don't want to be a bother. Do you know how to twerk? I like doing that. It's so funny. Look how I do it. I'm pretty good."

Noma turned around and started popping her booty up and down. Chloe laughed. She said, "I've never tried."

"Oh, well. Come on and try it. It's fun. I make videos sometimes. Guys like it. Do you have a boyfriend? I had one but we broke up before I came here. He was kind of a jerk anyway. But I've made some videos since I got here and a lot of guys like it."

"I don't think I want to make any videos."

"It would be fun. We could do it together sometime.

Really. I think—"

Chloe put her hand up halting the girl's speech. She said, "I'll think about it. Why don't you get comfortable and come down stairs when you're out of that silly uniform? Rebecca should be home soon and I'm sure she would like to talk to you when she gets here."

"You think I should change? She might want me to wear the uniform. I don't want to upset her. I need the job really bad. If I didn't have this place, I'd have nowhere to go. I might even have to go back to my momma's empty-handed. I really want to be successful."

"Don't worry, sweetie. I'll let her know that I told you to change."

"I'm sorry. You didn't tell me your name. I really like you. I know the other lady's name is Grace. What's your name?"

"I'm Chloe."

"Thanks, Ms. Chloe."

"No, please. Just call me Chloe."

"Oh, okay. I try to have manners. I don't want to offend anyone. I don't like to make enemies. I just want friends. Do you know what I mean?"

"I know exactly what you mean. I'll be your friend. First, get changed and meet me downstairs with Grace."

"Yes, Ms., I mean—Okay, Chloe."

37

Chloe and Grace were laughing together in the living room about an old memory from when they were in high school, when Noma came down stairs. Both women stopped to take in the petite figure of a girl in her short pink shorts and pink halter top. The young girl wasn't shy about showing off her body.

Noma said, "I hope this outfit is okay. I don't have a lot. I could put my uniform back on if you want. I dress kind of skimpy. It's just how I like it. Most people don't mind, but men stare sometimes. Is it okay? I mean, I could take it off and put my uniform back on. It's up to you. This is how I like to dress." The girl was twirling a strand of her long dark hair around her finger.

Chloe said, "It's okay, sweetie. You dress how you want to. Just don't run around naked. We've got a small boy here."

"Oh, no. I wouldn't do that, Chloe. I just like skimpy clothes, so that's all I've got. I don't really have money to get new clothes. Do you really think it's okay? I know my butt's hanging out. She turned and poked her butt out. She said, "It's a nice one, right? All my girlfriends used to be so jealous because of the way it pokes out." She laughed. She said, "They call me bubble butt Noma back home."

Grace said, "Baby, look at this one." She stood and pulled her pajama pants below her butt. She said, "I know I've got a bubble."

Noma said, "You do! I like it. Mine looks really good in jeans."

Grace pulled her pants up and smirked at Chloe. Chloe said, "I don't think so. You two can see my ass when we go for a swim. I'm not flopping it out right now."

All three of them laughed and their laughter was interrupted by a tiny voice. Barry said, "I'm hungry."

Chloe turned red in the face. Noma said, "Hello little bear. What's your name?"

"I'm Barry. I'm hungry."

Noma leaned down to make eye contact with Barry. She said, "I'm Noma. Let's go find something to eat. I'm hungry, too." She put out her hand and when Barry took it Chloe was stunned.

Chloe watched them leave the living room and she bit her lip. Grace asked, "What do you think?"

Chloe said, "I like her."

38

Music played and Noma danced around the kitchen cleaning up breakfast bowls. Barry sat at the table watching her. When Rebecca showed up she was amused at the scene. The talkative girl she had hired had apparently warmed up quickly and Barry looked like he was developing a new crush. Rebecca felt a small twinge of jealousy, but she knew that if Barry had a crush on his caretaker he would be easier to handle. It was part of the reason she hired a young girl like Noma.

Neither Noma nor Barry had noticed her in the doorway watching them, so she wandered off to find Chloe and Grace. Nowhere to be found in the house, Rebecca returned to the kitchen and spoke over the music. She said, "Nice moves."

Noma froze. She turned around with a look of embarrassment on her face. She said, "I'm sorry. I like to dance when I clean. I hope it's not a problem. We were having a good time and no one else is in the house, so I didn't think the music would bother anyone. I can play something else if you want. I have all kinds of music, not just rap."

"It's fine, baby. Can you tell me where Chloe and

Grace are off to?"

"Oh, they went down to the guest house. They said they wanted to organize some things. I told them I'd watch Barry. It's no trouble. That's what I'm here for, right? I mean, to cook, clean and help take care of the children. I don't mind at all."

"Beautiful. I'm going down to the guest house with them and I'll be back to talk to you in a while. Has anyone showed you around the house?"

"I was shown my room and I like to explore, so me and Barry will look at the rest later. Barry likes hanging out with me, don't you, Barry."

Barry nodded his head. He said, "I like Noma."

Rebecca raised an eyebrow. She said, "Interesting. You think I made a good choice, Barry? You're going to spend a lot of time with her."

"Yeah. I like her. She's pretty."

Rebecca laughed. She said, "Beautiful. You have a fan, Noma. I'll see you in a minute."

Rebecca left through the back door in the direction of the guest house. She could see Chloe and Grace sitting on the couch through the glass doors when she approached. They were sipping wine and talking. Rebecca opened the door and both women smiled at her arrival.

Chloe said, "Come sit down, Becca."

Rebecca sat in the chase lounge. She said, "We should start talking about how we're going to get your daughter, Grace."

Grace said, "I don't know if I'm ready."

Rebecca said, "You had years to prepare. Time to pull the trigger."

Chloe said, "She wants to learn self-defense, Becca. I do, too. Can you teach us?"

"I'm putting Barry in self-defense classes this week. You two can attend with him."

Chloe said, "I wanted you to teach us." She bit her lip.

"We'll go over some things at home, but if you really want to learn, you need to take some classes for the basics. Trust me, baby."

"I do."

"Beautiful. Now, Grace. We go see a lawyer tomorrow. There's paperwork to sign and I think the first step is a divorce, then a custody battle. Are you up for that?"

Grace looked like she was in another world. She jolted out of her daze, and said, "Whatever you think we need to do, Rebecca."

39

The school yard, crowded with young girls and specked with teachers, was pulsing with life when Rebecca arrived after school. She parked her Lexus and waited. Mila spotted her and ran to the car with three friends in tow. Poking her head in the car, Mila was excited to introduce her new friends to Rebecca. The girls were all polite and giddy. Mila said her goodbyes and climbed into the car.

She said, "Aunt Becca! I love this school!"

Rebecca said, "Beautiful. It's nice you made friends so quick."

"Yeah, everybody wanted to know about me. I didn't tell them everything, only that I just got back from Cancun and my aunt is rich." Mila giggled.

"Baby, you don't want people to like you because you have money."

"I know. I didn't want to tell them about my daddy, though. I don't want people to be my friend because they feel sorry for me."

"I guess you have a point, baby. You know when you make friends with someone you should feel comfortable being honest with them about what happened."

"I'll be honest. I just don't know them well enough.

We are rich, right?"

"We have more money than most people, but I'm sure that a lot of these girls have well off families. You want to stand out for your personality and charisma, not your parent's bank account."

"You are my parent, right? I mean, you're like my mom?"

"I'm your legal guardian. Your mother is still your mother."

"I think of you like my mom. But I'll just call you aunt Becca so I don't hurt mommy's feelings. I'm glad you love us."

"Beautiful."

40

At home, Rebecca found Barry sulking in his room. She walked in quietly and sat next to him on the floor. He was holding a tattered teddy bear. His eyes were glistening like he was on the very edge of crying. She rubbed his back and listened to him breathe for a moment.

He said, "My poppa gave me dis bear. He was a good Poppa."

Rebecca said, "I know you miss him."

"I do. An' it was my fault."

"It wasn't your fault. You didn't know what would happen."

"I jus' thought I would get in trouble I dinnit think poppa would die."

He put the bear down and went to the corner of the room and wiped his eyes. He said, "I know momma thinks it's all my fault. She doesn't even talk to me no more. I'm being good an' everything."

Rebecca stood and put her hair back. She said, "Tomorrow we start learning. Are you ready to start learning?"

"I still wanna go to regular school."

"I know. Let's try to do it from home for a while. Me and Noma can teach you. You like us, don't you?"

"Yes."

"Beautiful. Give us a chance and next year we'll talk about public school. Like we talked about. We have a deal, right?"

"Yes. I have to get good grades and behave."

"That's right, baby boy. Get ready for dinner. We're going to eat in a little while."

"Okay."

41

Chloe lay in her bed and couldn't find sleep. It was like she was suffocating. She could see Peter's face and the smile he wore seconds before the gun shot. Her thoughts would drift from Peter to the man she shot. Wishing the visons would stop she turned in the bed and put her face in the pillow to scream. Nothing worked to ease her torment and she hated it.

Climbing out of bed she went to the bathroom and opened her pill cabinet. She found the bottle of Xanax and opened it to inspect the contents. Pouring them out in her hand she counted. There were twenty-four of them. The thought of taking them all chided her to act and sleep forever. Dumping the pills back in the bottle, keeping one, she shook her head and looked at herself in the mirror. She could see the misery in her own eyes like a dark plague eating away at her soul.

Suicidal thoughts often plagued her now, and seldom a night went by when she didn't contemplate ending her life. She placed the pills back in the cabinet; they ticked against each other, taunting her. One lonely pill remained in her palm and she drew herself a glass of water to attempt sedating herself. The thoughts wouldn't win today. She wasn't leaving yet, she told herself.

Her heart was a kickdrum when she laid back in the bed and closed her eyes. She could still see the scenes that haunted her, like a horror movie on the backs of her eyelids. Tears spilled from her eyes like individual victims running from a tormentor. The bed felt like a prison. She looked over at her bedside clock and read 1:15 a.m. with a grimace.

Again, she climbed out of bed, making her way down stairs. The house was as quiet as a tomb. She went to the kitchen and opened the refrigerator. Chocolate milk called to her in the moment and she poured herself a half glass. Beyond her restlessness, Chloe wished she could sleep forever and those thoughts chilled her to the core. She finished her glass of milk and put it in the sink after a rinse.

Hesitant to go back to her room, she went to Rebecca's room and tried the knob. The door opened and Rebecca sat up in the bed. Rebecca asked, "Who's there? Is that you, Chloe?"

Chloe stepped in and closed the door behind herself. She said, "It's me. I couldn't sleep and was wondering if I could lay down with you."

Rebecca pulled her covers to the side. She said, "Sure, baby. Come get in."

Chloe crossed the room and climbed in the bed. She laid on her side and Rebecca put her arm around her. Rebecca asked, "Did you have bad dreams again?"

"I don't think I even slept, but I can't stop my mind from thinking about that day."

"Don't worry, baby. I'm here for you."

"Thank you, Becca. I feel horrible, like a baby. It was a good one, you know. Hiring a 'maid-slash-nanny'. Always with the surprises."

"Baby, you can be a baby. I'm going to take care of you."

In Rebecca's arms Chloe found the sleep she desired.

42

After dropping Mila off at school, Rebecca went to a local car lot and looked at SUV's. She'd been shopping for an Escalade with third row seating on the internet and there was one she liked with all the options at the big lot. She'd planned for this visit with a salesman and he was happy to see her arrive. Before she could get all the way through the front doors, she was approached. Seconds later, the salesman was ready to show her the vehicle of her choice.

After paying for the vehicle and delivery to her shop, she drove away in the Lexus smiling. Now she would have a family vehicle big enough to fit everyone. There were so many things to do and she didn't want to have to take multiple cars for everything. When she pulled in the circle drive of her new home, her phone rang.

The man's voice on the phone said, "We have another job."

"Beautiful. Where's the checkpoint?"

"Strainers bar. Eleven o'clock tomorrow night. Bring the equipment for a wet situation."

"I can do that. I'll be there."

She hung up the phone and took her seatbelt off. The

seat motor whined as she leaned it back to stare out of the sunroof. The jobs had always been her life. Investing legal money and accumulating wealth had been a hobby since she was a teenager, but the jobs—the jobs were her life. Nothing gave her greater pleasure, until she'd met Chloe and the children.

While Rebecca reclined, soft classical music played through her car stereo speakers and she closed her eyes. The feeling was serene and it wasn't long before she heard the rumble of her Chevy. She sat up in her seat and exited the vehicle to meet the delivery men. After inspecting the big black and pink monster she signed off on the work and delivery. The truck was nice and shiny like it had just rolled off the showroom floor. The loud exhaust had drawn a crowd. Noma and Barry were standing under the front door arch and when the delivery men were gone they approached.

Noma said, "This is a huge truck. I've never been inside of something that big. Can I drive it? Is it yours?"

Rebecca raised an eyebrow. She asked, "Where would you drive it?"

"Shoot, I'd drive it everywhere." The girl twisted a strand of her hair around a finger and cocked her hip to the side. She said, "You won't let me drive it, right? I'm a good driver. I wouldn't run no one over."

Barry said, "She don't like no one drivin' it."

Rebecca said, "That's right, Barry. Where's your mother?"

Noma said, "Oh, Chloe's sleeping in your bed. Grace is in the pool. Me and Barry were playing Jenga. Do you want to play? We can start a new game. We don't mind. Do we, Barry?"

Noma put her hand out and Barry took it. Rebecca said, "I might play later. You two finish your game and then we have to work on some of Barry's school lessons."

"Okay, Ms. Rebecca. We'll be ready. Should I come get you when we're done with our game?"

"No. I'll find you."

"Oh, Ms. Rebecca. I have to go to school tonight. You said you'd give me a ride to and from, right? When you hired me? Remember I told you I don't have a car and I'd need a ride? I have night school. Well, I know you probably remember, but can you give me a ride?"

Rebecca looked at Noma curiously. She said, "Yes, I remember. I'll give you a ride. How long will you be there?"

"From seven until ten. I hope I'm not a burden."

"You're not. It will be fine, just let me know when you're ready."

Rebecca went into the house and straight to her room. Chloe was balled up under the covers. Rebecca opened the curtains and Chloe moaned. When she approached the bed and sat on the edge, she felt sorrow for Chloe. What Chloe had gone through would probably never leave her. Rebecca knew she would always have the dreams and heartache. She rubbed Chloe's back gently.

Rebecca said, "Do you want some breakfast, baby?"

Chloe said, "I just want to sleep."

"It's almost noon, baby. How about you get up and

shower and we can go out for lunch."

Chloe turned over on the mattress and looked Rebecca in the eyes. She bit her lip. She asked, "Can it just be us? We haven't spent hardly any time alone."

"Sure, baby. Let me start Barry on his first lesson with Noma and we can go. I'll be ready by the time you are."

"Okay, Becca. I'll get up."

43

Rebecca and Chloe sat at the quaint diner that served all day breakfast just a few miles from the house. The sparsely occupied establishment boasted truckers and waitresses that smelled like they took smoke breaks often and served with crooked smiles. Rebecca took a sip of her sweet tea and watched Chloe mix sugar and creamer into a cup of coffee. It was curious to Rebecca that someone so beautiful could be so sad. She understood Chloe's anguish, but thought it was a shame for someone as gorgeous as Chloe to do anything other than smile and laugh all day long. When Chloe noticed her staring, she quit stirring her coffee and rolled her eyes.

Chloe asked, "What is it, Becca?"

"I was just observing you. I need to talk to you about tomorrow."

"What about tomorrow?"

"I have a job. I'll be leaving tomorrow morning after I drop Mila off for school. I won't be back for two days."

Chloe frowned. She asked, "What kind of job?"

"I'm not sure yet. I wanted to let you know, though."

"Can I go with you?"

"Interesting. Why would you want to do that?"

Rebecca peered at Chloe with her signature carnivorous curious look, rising an eyebrow.

Chloe said, "I can do burglary. You can teach me."

"I don't think so, baby. There's more to it than that."

"Like what?"

"I can't go into it, baby. If you want to do a private job, maybe we'll find one, but I don't always work alone and this job requires a very private team of professionals."

"You didn't tell me you worked with other people."

"Sometimes I do. That's all you need to know about it, though. For your protection."

"They would hurt me?"

"Let's not talk about it anymore. You haven't touched your coffee and I want a drink. Let's eat and then go scouting the local bars. I know where there are a few in this area that I haven't been to in a while."

"You're so bad, Becca."

"I like to drink a little, so what."

"I mean everything. You have all this money, you beat men up, you're a cat burglar and God only knows what else you do."

"Well. I invest in real estate all over the country in several different niches and I put money in index funds that I don't plan on touching for eleven more years, not that I need it. I don't know. I do a lot. Does it bother you?"

"No. I just don't know why you didn't tell me any of it sooner."

"Everything happens in its own time. Do you think I

should rattle off all my hobbies, accomplishments and bank holdings to everyone I meet?"

"You know I'm not saying that."

"Baby, I'm telling you now, and I rarely tell anyone my business."

Chloe bit her lip. She said, "Let's order and go get those drinks."

44

The first homeschool lesson went well and Noma knew how to teach Barry in a fun way. The two of them joked and laughed about the numbers and letters. When they had put everything away they turned music on and Noma talked Barry into dancing with her. Barry hadn't ever danced before and he laughed at Noma when she started being goofy, shaking her body and doing funny moves that all had some silly name. It had always been a difficult task to make Barry laugh and Noma had all the right moves to bring it out of him. He even enjoyed letting go and doing some of the funny dances with her.

Barry said, "You're alotta fun."

Noma said, "I know. I'm goofy. Do you want to go swimming? Do you know how to swim? I like getting in the pool. Especially on a hot day. What do you think? Do you want to go swimming?"

"Yeah, we can do that."

"Where's your bathing suit?"

"I'll find it. I can dress."

"Okay. I'm gonna change and we can meet at the pool. Don't get in without me, though. You should never get in the pool without an adult. You could drown. You don't want that and neither do I, so wait for me, okay?"

"Okay. I'll wait if you're not there."

Noma was the first outside and she sat on the edge of the pool with her legs dangling in the water, waiting for Barry. When he did come out she could she his shorts were on backwards. She laughed to herself and didn't mention it to him. He came to sit next to her. She put her hand out and he took it.

Barry said, "I wish I had known you before."

"Before what?"

"Before my poppa died. You make me feel normal."

Noma didn't know what to say. The way he said what he said made her heart ache. She squeezed his hand. Grace came out of the pool house. She wore her string bikini and looked like a supermodel with her defined long legs and smooth dark complexion. Her skin was bronzed to perfection from all the sun she'd been getting and Noma took a lingering look to admire her.

Grace asked, "What are you two up to? Are you going to get in the pool again, bubba?"

Barry said, "I'm thinkin' about it."

"Have you used the bathroom?"

Barry scowled. Noma said, "I'm sure he's not going to use the bathroom in the pool." She looked at Barry. She asked, "You won't do that, will you? That's gross."

Grace asked, "Have you used the bathroom, Barry?" With the type of tone that demanded an answer.

Barry stood and flipped her off. Grace said, "Watch it, bubba."

Barry turned and stomped his way up to the house.

Noma asked, "Are you coming back?"

Grace said, "Don't worry about him. He's just embarrassed. He shouldn't be gettin' in the pool unless he used the bathroom, though. He had an accident already."

Noma frowned. She said, "You embarrassed him. You could have been nicer. You know he has a crush on me."

"Well. I'd rather him be embarrassed then to have to clean another turd out of pool."

Noma stood and headed up to the house to console Barry. When she entered, she heard glass break. She rushed to Barry's room and found him trembling with a look of hatred on his face. His lamp was on the ground in pieces. Noma walked up to him and put her hand on his shoulder. He shrugged and she withdrew.

He asked, "Why are you in here?"

"I'm worried about you. Are you okay? I think Grace could have come at you different. I'm sorry if you're embarrassed. We all have accidents. When I was your age I had accidents. It's no big deal. Do you want to play Jenga or something? I'll clean up this mess and we'll tell your aunt Rebecca that we broke it pillow fighting. You won't get in trouble. We could still swim if you want. I don't care about anything anyone has to say about you. I like you. You don't have to be embarrassed."

Barry said, "Jus' leave. I don't wanna play with you. I wanna be alone."

"Oh, well, at least let me clean this mess. You can sit right there on the bed while I do it if you want."

Barry sat on the bed with his scowl screwed in place. Noma started cleaning the mess and became conscious of the bikini she was wearing. She looked back and Barry was watching her with the same scowl. She had the largest pieces of the destroyed item in hand. She smiled, stood, and cocked her hip.

She said, "I've got to get a dust pan, broom and trash bag for the rest of this mess. Don't get up and walk around because the little pieces suck when they get stuck in your foot. I'm going to put some shorts on real quick, too. Will you sit there and wait for me for a second? I'll only be a sec."

Barry continued to scowl in silence. Noma said, "I'll take your silence as a yes. You and me are still friends, right? I like being your friend. Well, I'm gonna do what I need to do. I'll be back in a sec."

When she left the room, Noma started thinking of ways she could make Barry smile again. She put her shorts on and found the cleaning materials. When she returned to the room Barry was lying on the bed staring at the ceiling. Noma cleaned the mess and went to discard the trash.

An idea formed and Noma went to the house library to browse. Rebecca had a lot of books and there were a couple of shelves for Mila and Barry. After reading a few titles, Noma settled on one called 'The Angry Alligator'. It looked well-worn and she thought that it might get Barry out of his funk.

When she returned to Barry's room he was lying on his side facing the wall. Noma walked up and cleared her throat. He didn't budge. She said, "I found a book in the library. Is it one of yours or is it one of your sisters? It's called 'The Angry Alligator'. It looks like someone read it a lot. Maybe it's a good book. Do you know it?"

Barry said, "My poppa got that book for me."

"Oh, did he read it to you?"

"My poppa used to. Sometimes my momma."

"Can I get in bed with you and read it? I can sit across the room in the chair if you want. I'll make voices and everything. It'll be fun."

"You can get in my bed if you want."

Noma climbed in the bed and Barry turned over on his back. Noma asked, "Are you ready?"

"Yeah."

"Arnold the alligator was always angry…"

45

The house stood quiet when Chloe and Rebecca entered. They found Grace sitting on the living room couch reading and Noma was dusting the television entertainment center. Rebecca asked, "Where's Barry?"

Noma turned from what she was doing, smiled and cocked her hip. She said, "He's asleep. He's so adorable. I read him a book and he fell right to sleep. He was upset this afternoon and I think it took a lot out of him."

Chloe said, "Wow. He rarely takes naps. You're good."

Grace said, "He'll be back up terrorizing everyone shortly. Where have you two been?"

Rebecca said, "In conference."

Grace said, "I've gotta get a job or I'll go crazy."

Chloe said, "How about we open a bottle of wine and sit around gabbing?"

All the women were open to that suggestion. Noma being nineteen was limited to one tall glass. They sat in the living room and sipped the sweet white wine, a 1998 Veuve Cliquot La Grande Dame that Rebecca thought everyone would enjoy. Chloe smiled at Grace, and Grace took a gulp.

Grace asked, "What is it Chloe?"

"I want to hear about your adventures. How you met Samuel and ended up in Cancun."

"Well, I was stripping at a hole in the wall club that didn't make me fill out an application or photocopy my ID. I guess they were like that because it wasn't full of ten's if you know what I mean. I got a lot of business there."

Noma asked, "You stripped?" She giggled. "I wouldn't have guessed that."

"Honey, don't judge a book by its cover. I stripped and I stripped good."

Chloe said, "Go on."

"Well, I met a guy that could do fake ID's and shit like that, so I got all new paper work. Then I started doing dope and someone brought me to Samuel's house to score. He was infatuated with me and I started talking to him a lot on the phone, then I was living with him, then I started to travel to Mexico with him to meet all these big-time dope dealers. I just looked pretty, he did all the talking. It was all good to me because I was living under a false name. Nobody checks the dope dealer's girlfriend's ID too close." Grace laughed. "I'm gonna miss it."

Noma asked, "Where'd you strip? I did it when I turned eighteen, but not for long. I didn't like all those men's hands on me every day. Even though I only did it for like a week, everyone in my town thinks I'm a slut. It sucks the way people judge you. I never slept with anyone from the club." She frowned.

Rebecca raised an eyebrow. She said, "Interesting.

That wasn't revealed to me."

"Oh, I don't tell many people about it."

Grace said, "I stripped in Atlanta, Georgia. The club was wild, but I didn't have to do it long either."

Rebecca said, "I don't think I could do it."

Chloe giggled. She said, "I don't know. I saw your moves, Becca. You'd probably make a good stripper."

"Baby, I'm a dancer, but I don't take my clothes off for money."

Noma said, "Some of us really need money. I don't want to do it again, but I probably would if I had to."

Barry walked into the room rubbing his eyes. He asked, "Can I have Kool-Aid? I'm thirsty, Noma."

Noma put down her glass. She said, "Come on, big boy. Let's get it together."

She left the living room hand in hand with Barry. Chloe said, "She's different, but she sure is good with Barry."

Rebecca said, "She's had a lot of practice raising her siblings. That's one of the reasons I hired her."

Grace said, "It was a surprise. You just do what you please."

"That's the way it should be, baby. You girls hang tight a while and I'll show you some things that will make it where you can do whatever you want, too."

There was a knock at the door. Rebecca said, "That must be the Escalade."

Chloe rolled her eyes and giggled. She said, "Here we go again."

"Baby, you heard Grace. I do what I want." She

winked at Chloe and went to answer the door.

When she returned, she was holding the keys to the new SUV. Everyone gathered outside and looked over the shinning silver luxury vehicle. Rebecca said, "This one's a community ride. I'm going to hang the key by the door and anyone can take it. Noma, you can drive yourself to school and back and use it to run household errands. Grace, you can go out during the day and try to find work or whatever other errands you want to run. I suggest that you and Noma communicate about the use because you two will need it most. Other than that, it's for when we all want to go out together."

Chloe said, "You think of everything."

"Baby, we have to be able to function."

46

The wall safe at Rebecca's apartment opened silently on its well-greased hinges. Making the decision to keep the place had really benefited her. Soon she would transfer the remaining contents of the apartment to the new home, but for now she wanted to keep 'the business' separate. She pulled the nine-millimeter equipped with suppressor from the safe and put it in her small duffle along with a set of lock picks and all black attire. The thought of Mila's smile when she had been dropped off at school that morning brought a smile to Rebecca's face. Time for business.

The drive to Strainers Bar was only a short distance from the apartment. The establishment stood deserted and closed for any would-be wandering clients. Rebecca parked in back and used her own key at the alleyway entrance. When she entered, the interior of the bar was dark, as usual. She made her way to a small room down a narrow hallway. Inside the room was her henchman, Griffin.

Griffin grinned a toothy smile, showing upper and lower rows of diamond encrusted gold teeth. He said, "Damn, boss. Vacation done you fuckin' good. When you gonna let me hit that shit?"

Rebecca raised an eyebrow. She said, "Baby, you better be talking about weed."

"Come on, boss. You know I fuck wit' you. I'm just juggin'."

"You better have called me here for more than just a chance to get on my nerves."

Rebecca sat in the chair opposite Griffin. Griffin said, "I got this for you."

He passed an envelope to her and she pulled out the contents. Her pulse quickened. Someone was ordering a hit and the picture in front of her showcased Grace, at the beach with a smile on her face.

47

"Make us a couple of drinks, Griffin. I'll take a dry martini."

Griffin exited the room and Rebecca read the short note with the picture. It read, 'Name: Grace Austin. Last known destination: Dallas, Texas with one Chloe Apple. She may use an alias. She has a child she may visit in Chicago, Illinois. Status: Missing. The body should not be found.'

'Status: missing' meant they had no idea where she was yet. Rebecca was infuriated that Chloe's name had been mentioned. When Griffin returned with the drinks, Rebecca sipped hers and looked Griffin in the eyes. She said, "We're going to do something a little different on this job, Griffin."

Griffin furrowed his brow. He said, "Whatever you want, boss. Tell me w'at you mean by different."

"I want you to find out who ordered this hit."

"Dat shit's easy. Some drug dealer in Atlanta."

"Find out his location and contact me with the info. After I get his address, and I go to Atlanta, I want you to confirm the hit and set up a meeting for the final payment."

Griffin took a bundle of cash from a bag on the table. He said, "Here's the first half of yours, ten thousand."

"Keep it."

Griffin smiled his golden grin. He said, "My pleasure, boss. Give me an hour and meet me here. I'll have all the info you need. Are you gonna nail him?"

"I'm going to pin him to the wall, Griffin."

48

With the information on one Samuel Lagos, and an untraceable car ready to go, Rebecca went home to talk to Chloe and Grace. She thought of different ways she could get them to stay in the house for the weekend. Samuel Lagos of Atlanta, Georgia was a threat that had to be dealt with swiftly.

Music pumped through the house and Rebecca felt unhinged by the news she'd received. Chloe, Grace and Noma were all in the living room acting crazy. They danced around and when they realized Rebecca was watching them they stopped. Chloe brushed her hair from her face.

Chloe asked, "What's wrong, Becca?"

Rebecca said, "There's an issue I can't explain right now. I need you all to stay in the house until Monday. Noma, did you go to the grocery store?"

"Yeah, I went. I bought a lot with the card you gave me. I hope you don't mind. I put the receipt in the box you told me to put them in. I guess I shouldn't have went shopping hungry. A cute guy helped me load them. He was like my age. I hope I didn't spend too much."

Rebecca said, "Don't worry about it, baby. You all

need to stay in the house until Monday and if I'm not back by then, Mila can't go to school Monday. I'll call if anything changes."

Chloe asked, "Where are you going?"

"To solve the problem, baby."

Grace said, "I was going to look for a job."

"Baby, that'll have to wait. Tell me that you will all stay home over the weekend."

Chloe said, "We'll stay home, Becca."

"Beautiful. Noma, I need a ride to the mall."

"Oh, I like shopping."

Rebecca raised an eyebrow. She said, "I'm sure you do. You're not going in. I'm getting picked up there. I don't want you to go inside."

"I won't."

Rebecca gave Noma her signature curious stare. She said, "Interesting. A short answer. You shouldn't lie to me, Noma. Not if you like staying here."

"Oh, I do. I'm not lying. I won't go inside. I'll drop you off and come right back. You know I was thinking about the guy at the grocery store, though. He was so cute."

"Baby, you let that go for now. There'll be plenty of time for boys later."

"Oh, okay. I won't worry about it. I really want a boyfriend, though. Would that be okay? When you get back?"

Barry walked in the room and yawned. He said, "Noma, I'm tired. Will you read to me?"

Noma giggled. She said, "Okay, big boy. Let's go pick

a book."

She took Barry's hand and they left the living room. Rebecca said, "Chloe, Grace, promise me you won't leave."

Grace said, "For Heaven's sake. You're starting to scare me."

"Baby, it's not a joke."

"I don't know what kind of stuff you're into, but if Chloe promises, so do I."

Chloe rolled her eyes. She said, "Another freakin' adventure. I promise, Becca. We won't go anywhere."

49

After being dropped at the mall, Rebecca waited and watched the crowd. She used her throw away phone and called a cab. A car was waiting for her in a parking lot not far away. It was an unremarkable white Nissan Maxima with tinted windows. She used the key Griffin gave her and in minutes she was on the highway, traveling light but heavy. She had allowed herself plenty of time to make it to Atlanta. A room waited for her in Decatur, the part of Atlanta where Samuel Lagos kept his main residence.

Fourteen hours of No-doze and non-stop driving ushered in the new day as Rebecca parked in the modest hotel's parking lot where a reserved room awaited her. She wore a blond wig and dressed conservatively when she checked in under her alias. The overweight flunky at the service counter didn't pay her much attention. Rebecca laughed to herself when she entered the room. She thought that the clerk must have been gay. She looked at her butt in the mirror. It was amusing. He would not likely remember her bubble.

She put her bag on the bed and removed the silenced nine-millimeter. She would make the call, then get some rest. By tomorrow morning, Samuel Lagos would no longer be an issue. She mused how the newspapers and media would likely call the homicide a drug deal gone bad. It was obvious to her why he ordered the hit. Most drug dealers were paranoid when a spouse or lover left them and he likely thought that Grace knew too much. She smiled into the phone as she called Griffin. The man had paid to be executed.

When Griffin answered, Rebecca said, "Call the deer and tell him to have breakfast at Yellowbirds Bagel in North David Hills 2023 Clairmont Rd. Ten a.m. I'll intercept."

"Check that."

Rebecca sat on the edge of the bed and stared at herself in the mirror. She could never figure out exactly why her work turned her on so much. Samuel would never taste another bagel, if he liked them at all. The thought of killing him made her nipples hard.

Rebecca set her alarm to wake her in four hours and dozed off.

50

Grace and Chloe sunbathed by the pool. Grace asked, "What do you think is going on with Rebecca? Why would she want us to stay home all weekend? She sounded so urgent and stern."

Chloe said, "She has her reasons, Grace. Believe me, if she says we need to stay in she has a good reason."

"I don't know if I trust your girlfriend, Chloe. She's a little strange."

"We're all strange, Gracie."

"That's true. There's just something different about her."

"She's different alright."

"Gross. Did you just make a sexual innuendo?"

"Don't worry about it, Gracie. Everything will be fine."

"I hope so. I don't want to be trapped by the pool sipping margaritas the rest of my freakin' life." She winked at Chloe and they both had a little laugh.

51

When the alarm went off, Rebecca felt like she had slept for days. You might think she would have nightmares about some of the things she'd done. On the contrary, Rebecca always found it easy to sleep, and her sleep was an abyss, a dark and comforting dreamless abyss. She looked at herself and grinned. It was time to observe her next victim's movements. A part of the job she looked forward to. There was something about watching someone that didn't know they were being watched. She remembered watching Chloe after they had first met. Becoming consumed with the beautiful woman and almost ignoring the real reason she'd taken the job at Puff's Bakery.

Her obsession with stalking prey had led her to many places and revealed the most interesting things about people. It would be hard to ignore her impulses. When someone offended her, there was even more pleasure in the hunt, usually. Being paid to do it was a thrill, especially when she occasionally let a contracted victim see her face before she did the deed, they didn't always recognize her. Other times she had played some minor role in their lives. Something about that recognition made the kill more exciting and savory for her.

A glance at her monitor, with a well-placed camera in the window, showed the parking lot to be deserted except for a young couple loading their luggage and a baby in their car to depart. Rebecca watched them until they left and then scanned the rest of the parking lot. Although she was disguised well, she didn't want many people to see her leave the room where she would have to return for the night.

When it was clear, she loaded into the car with her equipment. She always brought her equipment in case there would be an unforeseen opportunity. The drive to Samuel's home wasn't far. A nice suburban neighborhood. Kids playing in yards. There were dumps along the way, but the place seemed family oriented. All except Samuel's home. It was a dick of a bachelor's pad. After parking, a few houses down, she observed three women leaving and before they pulled away another car showed up. Rebecca thought to herself that he was a popular prick.

After about an hour, she spotted Samuel on the porch drinking a beer with the man who had arrived after the girls left. She watched them through binoculars and the dark haired, greying and balding tan man was definitely her target. She had not seen him in Cancun, but the picture she had of him matched. She wondered what Grace was doing with such a douche. She smiled thinking of what she was going to do to him.

The man visiting left and Rebecca drove past the home to get a good look at Samuels car. It was a pristine

80's model Mercedes-Benz. Her plan hatched and on the way to the hotel she stopped off at a drive thru liquor store to get a bottle so she could celebrate the soon to be dead man's upcoming funeral.

Rebecca called Griffin as soon as her room's door closed. She said, "Griff, call and make the arrangements."

"No sweat, boss. I'm on that shit."

"Beautiful."

52

Griffin called confirming the meet up at Yellowbirds Bagels. Rebecca cleaned and oiled her pistol in anticipation of the morning. She opened her bottle of tequila and used one of the hotel's plastic cups as a shot glass. The burn felt good and the warm feeling in her gut wasn't just from the tequila. She laid back on the bed and felt herself.

When morning came, Rebecca was up at dawn. She prepared and dressed. After cleaning the room so it would be hard to find any physical evidence of her there, she looked in the mirror and admired herself in all black with the blonde wig. She mused that she could have been an actress. She'd spent her whole life a chameleon. The big screen couldn't have brought her the joy she gained from her work, though. Nothing but blood could satisfy the urge for as long as she could remember. It started with animals and transitioned into what she had become. There were no regrets for Rebecca. She felt no remorse.

Chloe made her feel. She wasn't sure how much she liked that. Life was simpler when there was no one to care for. There were no regrets to be had, either. She loved Chloe. An anomaly. She wasn't even sure she really loved her father. The only person who ever knew her completly. Her mentor. The destroyer. Her father. The thought of Chloe seemed to lighten the load she carried, like a ton of bricks in her chest somehow being lifted one piece at a time every day she spent with her new companion.

When exiting the hotel, she felt sure she hadn't been spotted. She left the room key inside on the bed and called in the checkout before leaving, so she didn't have to worry about seeing anyone else in the area face to face except her soon to be victim. After parking across the street from Samuel's home, Rebecca checked her watch. Thirty minutes till ten.

It wasn't long before Samuel left the residence in his dark green Mercedes. The jack off had the nerve to look happy and put down his convertible top. His music played loud enough that Rebecca could hear it with her windows up at stops. She bided her time and on the third stop sign, where the street seemed deserted, she bumped his car lightly. He threw his car in park and started slamming his fist into the steering wheel. Rebecca exited her vehicle swiftly. She approached his Mercedes with her pistol behind her.

He looked over his shoulder and yelled. He said, "You stupid, fucking bitch! This car's a classic! I don't have time for this shit you cunt!"

Rebecca asked, "Do you know Grace Austin?"

His alarmed look pleased her.

He began to exclaim, "What the .."

Rebecca released a quick and virtually silent round

from the nine-millimeter directly into his left eye socket. His brains covered the passenger side of the dashboard in clumps. Back in her vehicle, she left the scene swiftly. She looked in the rearview and laughed. She said to the fading image, "Fuck you and your classic."

When she entered the highway her adrenaline high began to ebb. She would be home not long after midnight and everything had gone smoothly. There was plenty of time to come up with an alibi for why she ordered everyone to shut in. She had a feeling that Chloe wasn't going to be easily satisfied, but for her protection she knew she would have to lie, if she could. Lying to Chloe felt disturbingly wrong to Rebecca.

53

The house was quiet when Rebecca arrived. She'd called Chloe when she was about an hour away. Chloe was the only one awake, waiting for her on the living room couch in a pink night gown, when Rebecca arrived. Rebecca walked up and sat next to her. She leaned over and gave Chloe a kiss.

Rebecca said, "The situation is resolved. No worries."

Chloe asked, "What was the situation?"

"It was nothing, baby. I don't want to talk about it."

"It had to be something. You left for two days and from what I gather we were in some kind of danger."

"The threat is over. We need to think of something to tell everyone. I've been racking my brain about it. I don't want to lie to you, but it's better if you don't know. Baby, I wouldn't be keeping secrets if it weren't necessary. You understand, right?"

"Are you going to tell me some day?"

"Baby, someday I'll explain everything. For now let's tell everyone that I had a disgruntled tenant making threats in Arizona and I wanted everyone inside and safe."

"What are we going to say he was disgruntled about?"

"That's it, baby. I like the way you think and I like that you trust me. We'll say I was evicting him and he made death threats. I couldn't take the chance that he was crazy enough to make the drive and do something, so I had to work with the authorities to see that he got what was coming to him and get him off my property."

"Okay. That's what we'll tell everyone and make sure they stay vigilant for suspicious people."

"Beautiful. You're better than I hoped."

"I'm tired is what I am. Do you want to get a bottle of wine and go to the room?'

"Baby, that depends what you want to do with the bottle." Rebecca winked.

"I don't know. I can be creative." Chloe rolled her eyes.

"Interesting."

"You're so bad, Becca."

54

Grace and Noma accepted the alibi and the household went back to the flow it had before. After Barry's lesson for the day, Rebecca went to Chloe and Grace. She said, "I want to go enroll Barry in martial arts today. It will give him more discipline and I've been recommended to a dojo. Barry can start with karate, and you two can start with Krav Maga. That's my suggestion."

Chloe asked, "What's Krav Maga?"

"It's the method of combat for the Israeli army. I've trained and it's a good place to start."

Grace said, "I trust you. After seeing you fight I'd take the flying duck class if you told me to." Grace laughed.

Rebecca said, "Baby, if they had a flying duck class I would have taken it by now. The more you learn the better equipped you are to handle sudden threats. We'll load up and go look at the facility."

55

The facilities were clean and professional, as Rebecca expected. It wasn't often that Griffin referred her anywhere that wasn't top of the line. They took a tour and Barry warmed quickly watching students and instructors in action. Rebecca timed their visit so that there would be a class going. Adults were sparring and the children's classes didn't start until later that day when the younger students would be out of school. It didn't matter that his class didn't start until the evening to Barry, and Rebecca suspected it wouldn't matter, as long as he could see some action in the meantime. The students and teachers were putting on a show and it wasn't hard to see that Barry felt thrilled to be there.

Grace and Chloe asked questions and Rebecca only interjected when she felt it was necessary. Chloe asked, "Will this be good for my son even though he's been violent?"

The instructor said, "Martial arts can be helpful in many aspects of life. It should increase his confidence and help him with self-discipline. After taking classes most parents report improved behavior."

Grace said, "I hope it can improve my behavior, Mr.

Baker. I'm a bad girl."

Chloe rolled her eyes. Leave it to Grace to hit on the instructor.

Rebecca said, "If you all like the facilities." She raised her eyebrow and looked at Grace. "And the staff, we can sign up today." She looked down at Barry. "What do you say? Barry?"

Barry said, "I want to do it. Can I start now?"

Rebecca looked at Mr. Baker. She asked, "Would it be okay for him to start this evening?"

Mr. Baker said, "Please, call me Trey. If you can, get him a karategi, and I'll let the children's instructor know to expect him this evening."

Grace asked, "What class do you teach?"

"I teach adults. The beginners class starts tonight, also. Maybe you should join us?"

"I will. If it's alright with Rebecca."

"Baby, it's fine by me, but we have to fill out paperwork and pay some fees first. Don't we, Trey? You lead the way."

After signing up the ride home was charged with energy. Chloe asked, "Shouldn't we enroll Mila?"

Rebecca smirked. She said, "Mila's going to learn from me."

Barry protested. He said, "I wanna learn from you."

"Beautiful. I like that you like to spend time with me, Barry. We spend a lot of time together and I want something to do with your sister. You understand, don't you?"

Barry scowled. He said, "I do. It's not fair, though."

"Not everything is, baby. Something you should be acquainted with by now. Let's not turn this into an argument."

"Yes, ma'am."

Chloe's mouth hung open from shock. She hadn't heard Barry willingly call anyone sir or ma'am without being prompted. Rebecca sensed her shock and looked over raising an eyebrow. Chloe rolled her eyes and turned the radio up. There was no use getting into it. Rebecca was obviously the boss and Chloe was enjoying the ride.

56

The whole bandwagon pulled up to Mila's school with the sun shining and blinging off the hood of the Escalade. They were all in a light mood. Chloe said, "I'm going to get out and get Mila. Where does she usually exit?"

Rebecca pointed to the doors the children would come out of and Chloe exited the vehicle. Rebecca admired Chloe's sun dress as her lover walked away and she felt sorrow for all Chloe had been through. She did her best to make her happy, but she knew she was still second and always would be to Peter.

Mila climbed in the truck excited. She said, "My friend Gabby is having a slumber party this weekend. Can I go, Aunt Becca?"

Rebecca said, "You need to ask your mommy, baby."

"I did and she said to ask you."

Rebecca looked at Chloe with curiosity. Chloe smirked and shrugged her shoulders. Rebecca wondered if Chloe would still love her if she knew who she really was. Rebecca shook her head and smirked.

Rebecca said, "It's Monday. If you do good all week in school and help Noma with a chore each night you can go."

Mila lit up. She asked, "What chore?"

"You can help her wash dishes or take out trash. Dust. There's a lot to do and I bet she'd appreciate the help. All you have to do is ask her what you can help her do each day you come home from school. Do we have a deal?"

"Heck yeah!"

Chloe laughed. She asked, "Where'd you get that word, Mila?"

"You mean, heck? Gabby says it all the time." Mila giggled.

When they made it home Mila scrambled out of the SUV and ran inside yelling for Noma. Chloe was amazed how good Rebecca was with the children. She followed the crowd inside grateful to have a makeshift family to spend her time with. Deep inside guilt pangs rose as she thought of Peter. Often, she hid her emotions because she didn't want everyone to know how much she was suffering. Things had moved quickly and she had to wonder if Peter was watching her at times. If he understood.

In the foyer, Mila ran to Chloe. She said, "I can't find her. I looked everywhere."

Chloe said, "Maybe she's in the pool or cleaning the guest house. Have you checked there?"

Mila turned without a word and ran for the back door. Chloe smiled at her enthusiasm. She found Rebecca and Grace in the living room cracking open a bottle of wine. The two drinkers had wine in common. It was an everyday occurrence and Chloe was beginning to enjoy it as much as they did.

Chloe sat on the couch next to Rebecca and Rebecca patted her leg. Grace began pouring them all glasses and then they heard a scream. The hairs stood on Chloe's arm. It was Mila's scream, coming from outside. A blood curdling sound. All three women stood erect, wine spilling everywhere, and Rebecca was the first in action heading for the door with Chloe right behind her.

When they stepped out back Mila was running up the walkway and stairs to the main house. She grabbed Chloe by the legs. She was trembling hard. Chloe asked, "What happened?"

"T-there's a m-man attacking Noma in the guest house!"

Rebecca ran for the pool house and entered swiftly. She was ready for a fight. What she found infuriated her. Noma and the new pool guy were scrambling to clothe themselves. Rebecca had the urge to attack them both. She turned without saying anything, to go console Mila.

Rebecca approached and knelt in front of Mila. She said, "It's okay, baby. She wasn't being attacked. She was just wrestling with the new pool guy."

Mila shuddered. She said, "They were naked, Aunt Becca. And she was making weird noises."

Rebecca was furious. She controlled her temper as well as she could. She said, "Sometimes adults wrestle like that because clothes get in the way. She was just making pretend noises."

Noma and the new pool guy approached. Noma said, "I'm really sorry. Me and James were getting along so well. It just kind of happened. I'm really sorry, Rebecca."

Rebecca stood to look her in the eyes. She said, "We will talk about this later."

Noma and James went to the main house. Rebecca said, "Mila. Let's get some ice cream. What do you think?"

Mila wiped her eyes. She said, "That was scary."

"I know it, baby. Let's get some ice cream and forget about it. Okay?"

"Okay, Aunt Becca."

57

Noma sat in tears in front of Rebecca, Chloe and Grace. She said, "I was just gonna make out with him and then we started to do it. I didn't think Mila would see us. I didn't think anyone would see us. I feel so bad. I don't wanna lose my job. I love you guys and the kids. It was a mistake. I don't know what to say to make it better."

Rebecca asked, "Ladies, what do you think we should do?"

Grace said, "I think we should give her another chance."

"Chloe, baby, what do you think?"

"I think she should be more careful. Mila may be scarred because of this and now I'm going to have to have the sex talk with her. I can't let her go to that slumber party thinking it's the thing to do, to wrestle naked when you like someone. There's no telling what kind of disaster that would cause."

Rebecca said, "We're going to let you stay, but next time you decide to bump your bottom with someone I would suggest you make sure you lock the door."

"Oh, I will. I'm so sorry. Do you guys hate me or look

at me different? I'm really not a slut. I hadn't had sex in a long time before James. I guess too long. I don't know what I was thinking. I'll be more careful."

Grace said, "We're not going anywhere for the rest of the night. Let's open some wine and get a buzz. You're joining us, Noma."

58

Rebecca sipped her wine slowly. She asked, "How was the first class at the dojo?"

Chloe said, "It was intense. I'm going to lose weight and tone up quick."

Grace laughed. She said, "You're already skinny and tone, Chloe. I'm the one who could lose a few pounds. The class was awesome and the instructor is a hunk. I'm ready to go back now."

Rebecca said, "I'm glad you're enjoying yourselves. Barry said he had fun. Did either of you watch him any?"

Chloe said, "I looked over there every now and then. He looked like he was getting into it. It's hard to tell with him sometimes because of those facial expressions. That scowl he wears makes you think he's mad when he's just fine."

Rebecca said, "He hasn't done that much lately."

Chloe rolled her eyes. She said, "I think he wants to be tough in class."

"Adorable. Do you think he made any friends?"

"I don't know, Becca. He talks to you more than me."

"He told me he didn't make any friends, baby. I'm just wondering if you observed him with anyone who could be his buddy. You know, he won't acknowledge it himself easily if he did."

Chloe said, "He did spar with one boy and I think he had a lot of fun. Wouldn't that be something? He's never had a friend."

Rebecca said, "I'm going to talk to Mila tomorrow and start training her soon. She likes the new school and that's good. Self-defense is important and I think it'll help us bond. Do you have any objections?"

"I'm okay with whatever you want, Becca."

"Beautiful. I want another glass of wine. How about you, girls?"

They filled their cups and the rest of the evening went with good company and a few bad jokes.

59

The pool house was fully furnished by the time Grace moved in. Rebecca and Chloe were helping decorate and Rebecca thought it was a good time to talk to Grace about Darla. Rebecca said, "The attorney called and said the divorce papers were being finalized. He said that we're going to have to go to court to get custody of Darla. Since you aren't asking for anything in the divorce, your ex signed pretty quick, but he doesn't want to give up Darla that easy."

"I'm as ready as I'm gonna be. I couldn't have done this without you."

Chloe asked, "How are things going with Trey? It's getting pretty serious, isn't it?"

Grace started biting her nails. She said, "It is getting serious. I think he's in love."

Chloe said, "That's a good thing. Right?"

Grace became conscious of her nail biting habit and pulled her hand away from her mouth. She said, "In some ways it is good. I just don't know if I'm ready to be serious about anyone. I was on the laptop the other day and I saw an older article. It was about that guy, Samuel. The one I was with in Cancun. He was shot to death last month. They say it was a drug deal gone bad. Found a bunch of money on him. It's weird to me that they didn't take the money, but apparently, he had it hidden good. I didn't realize that I had feelings for him."

Chloe said, "I'm so sorry, sweetie. We had no clue. Why didn't you say anything?"

Grace said, "I didn't want to bother you with it. He died too long ago to go to the funeral. He's already buried, and I guess I just thought it was pointless to bring it up, but I can't get it off my mind."

Rebecca felt frustration welling up inside herself. She wished she could tell Grace that Samuel had put a hit on her and that if it hadn't have come to her, then Grace would probably be dead and Samuel would still be riding around in his douche bag car. Instead she had to go along with the mourning process of her friend without saying a word. Exposing the truth wasn't an option.

Chloe said, "It's a good thing you came with us when you did. You might have been killed, too."

Grace's eyes filled with tears. She said, "Maybe you're right, honey. There's nothing I could have done. It's not like we were in love. It's just a shock."

Rebecca said, "That's understandable, but let's not let it take our eyes off our goals. Do what you have to do to mourn, I suggest a bottle of liquor, then we need to move forward."

Grace said, "That's a good idea. Let's make drinks."

Rebecca said, "We'll make whisky and coke. How does that sound?"

"It sounds perfect."

Chloe rolled her eyes. She said, "Leave it to you two to turn this into a reason to get sloshed."

Rebecca raised an eyebrow. She said, "I'm trying to help her cope." She smirked.

"Okay, Becca. Y'all are going to turn me into an alcoholic."

Grace said, "Honey, you drink every day now. You are an alcoholic, short stuff."

Rebecca said, "I'm serious about our business, Grace. We've got to focus on Darla."

Grace laughed. She said, "Okay, momma bear. I'm starting to feel better already, mix some drinks already."

"Baby, 'momma bear' will rip your head off to put it on straight."

Grace said, "Oh my God! Rebecca, you *are* crazy."

"You know it, baby."

60

When they pulled up to the martial arts studio, Trey happened to be standing out front. Barry and Chloe went inside and Grace stayed back to talk to Trey. His long blonde hair was free flowing and the scar on the left side of his face was accentuated in the sunlight. Grace had thoughts of swooning as she approached him. They were becoming very close and had even kissed. She desperately wanted him to ask her over to his place. She was tired of waiting.

Grace asked, "What are you doing tonight, Trey?"

"I don't know. I don't have any plans, I guess."

"How would you like to come to my house? It's not much. Just a pool house, but it's comfy."

"I think I can do that. You'll have to write down your address."

"What about if you gave me a ride home after class?"

"I don't know about that. I've got to shower and everything."

"You can shower at my place. We can get in the pool if you want. There's a hot tub."

"Okay. I'll take a shower in the studio locker room if you'll wait after class and we can leave after that."

Grace was a little disappointed. She thought she could seduce him fresh out of the shower. She said, "I don't mind waiting. Do you drink wine?"

"Not often, but yeah."

"Good. We can open a bottle and order take out. I've got movies. Do you want to watch one with me?"

"Sure. Let's get inside. It's about time for class."

Grace walked up and kissed him on the cheek. Then she turned to walk in front of him, hoping he would check out her butt. The way he looked into her eyes when he had stood face to face with her, she could tell he was falling for her. All she had to do now is close the deal. Sneaking kisses was fun, but as serious as it was getting, she wanted to go all the way. For someone as confident as he presented himself to be, it did concern her that she was making most of the moves. It was obvious he wanted the same thing she did, so if making the move had to be on her, so be it.

61

The guest house was dimly lit, Grace and Trey stretched across the couch, bodies intertwined and tongues mingling, waiting for the take out Chinese food to arrive. Grace's skin felt hot and it took everything she had to contain herself, she didn't want to go too far until Noma brought the food. Anticipation of pleasure coursed through her veins and from what she felt it was coursing through Trey's veins, also. Being in the moment felt surreal, pure ecstasy for Grace. She was so wrapped up in him that she knew she could unravel at any moment.

The knock on the door broke Grace from her trance. She took a sip of her wine and winked at Trey. She said, "You stay put. I'll be right back."

After the meal, they skipped the movie and consummated their relationship, again and again.

62

The main house bustled early morning despite it being the weekend. Grace came in through the back and Chloe smiled wide from the dining room table. Chloe said, "Come sit down. I've got some questions for you."

Grace sighed and sat down. She asked, "What is it, my nosey friend?"

"Well, you and Trey have been shacked up for two days ordering take out and doing God knows what. So. What have you been doing? Hmm?"

"Shut your mouth, woman. You're going to embarrass me. Besides, there's children running around."

Noma put a plate in front of Grace. There were bacon, eggs and toast. Grace smiled and took a bite. She said, "This is freakin' good, Noma."

"Oh, thanks. I'm sure you need to replenish your energy. I know I would if I spent days locked down with a man like that. How many—"

Grace interrupted the onslaught. She said, "Noma, please. I don't want to talk about it now."

Chloe whispered. She asked, "Is it big?"

Grace turned red in the face, a difficult thing to do with her dark complexion. She bit her fingernails. She spoke softly. She said, "He's huge."

The three of them laughed and Rebecca interrupted their laughter. She asked, "What did I miss?"

Noma scurried back into the kitchen area like she'd been scalded. Amused and curious Rebecca prodded. She said, "If no one wants to include me, I'll just have to throw you all out on your butts."

Chloe rolled her eyes. She said, "Such an obvious lie. We were just heckling Grace about her beef adventure."

Grace let her mouth hang open feigning offense. Rebecca said, "Interesting. We've all had a beef conquest or two. Haven't we?"

All the girls were blushing now. Chloe said, "You're horrible, Becca."

"Beautiful. Grace, I didn't want to interrupt you, but yesterday the lawyer called to confirm the court date on Monday. We'll go to Chicago tomorrow."

"I gotta check on that property in North Richland Hills, Sunday evening. Remember?"

"Baby, I remember I hired you to be the property manager for several properties. Do you know what that makes me?"

"I know. You're the boss. I was just looking forward to it. It's a nice property and if everything checks out we could make a bundle."

"There will be plenty of bundles to make, baby. Your daughter is more important and we have to be there for this one. You have to take the stand."

"Is there another way? I don't want to see Kevin."

"Baby, that's unavoidable. You are going to have joint

custody if things don't go all the way in our favor. He might get her for three months out of the year, or even six. We're trying to take her and minimize her exposure to him. I have a feeling he doesn't want her anyway, so this might be an easy win. I think the only reason he's resisting is to give you a hard time. I've been having him investigated and he isn't a very good father. More importantly, reports tell me that Darla doesn't seem happy. It's crucial that we are there, and prompt, and it is crucial you take the stand."

"I understand. I just hate that I have to see that jerk."

63

After the two-and-a-half-hour flight, Grace stretched her legs and yawned. She said, "I didn't plan on being back in Chicago ever again until today."

Rebecca said, "We all have to face our problems eventually. When this is over you'll be glad you did it."

"I think you're right. I do want Darla back, but I never imagined it could happen so soon. It's one thing to think about it and something totally different to do it. If it weren't for you and Chloe I don't think I could do it." Grace's eyes filled with tears. "I'm so grateful for you."

Rebecca had been hearing that a lot lately and it was beginning to make her feel appreciated more than she had been her whole life. She hugged Grace. She said, "I'm glad I can help, baby. Let's get our luggage and check into our room. I need a drink."

In the hotel near the airport, Grace pulled her shoes off and laid back on the bed. She said, "This place is pretty nice."

"We've got to practice what you're going to say in court, baby. Our lawyer has some questions he will ask and I'm sure his lawyer will counter. We have to be ready."

64

The court room was almost empty except for officers, the judge and lawyers. When Grace saw Kevin her skin crawled. It had been so long since she had seen him she'd almost forgotten what he looked like. She tried to forget, but she saw in his eyes the same hatred from years ago. He was in a cheap black suit and a wrinkled blue shirt with a pin-striped light blue tie. The same outfit he wore at his mother's funeral, just days before he almost beat her to death and she made her escape. Theirs was a loveless marriage for many years, and she had no feelings for the disheveled man. His green eyes sunk in his sockets with rings around them like he hadn't slept well for years. He shouldn't sleep well, from Grace's perspective. He was a monster, in her book, and she could never forgive him for what he did to her. Her insides turned when she thought of how she had abandoned Darla with the tormenter. He had no lawyer.

Rebecca said, "Let's have a seat. It's about to start."

The bailiff called for everyone to rise. He said, "All rise, the Honorable Judge Crates is presiding."

Afterwards everyone was asked to be seated and the session began. After formalities, Grace's lawyer stood and called Grace to the stand. He asked her name and about the date and incident to which she was to testify. Grace felt nervous tension and her palms began to sweat. She started to bring her hand to her mouth, then abruptly put it in her lap. When she stated her name and the date of the offense she was to expose, her voice trembled and she had to clear her throat.

Grace said, "We came home from his mother's funeral and he was upset about losing her and an incident where my friend's two-year-old son bit my daughter on the cheek. There was an exchange between my friend's husband and Kevin."

The lawyer asked, "Was there a physical altercation?"

"No. Not between the men, but when we returned home to Chicago, there was between us."

A tear escaped Grace's eye and she began to tremble. Doing her best to hold her composure, she gently wiped the tear from her cheek. The lawyer asked, "What kind of physical altercation occurred between you and Mr. Austin? Go into as much detail as you can remember Mrs. Martinez."

"I didn't want to aggravate him. He snapped every time I tried to speak to him on the ride home, all the way from Dallas to Chicago he was being verbally abusive. Several times he told me he should kick my ass for making him go to my friend's house. When we did get home, he blew up. Darla was asleep and I laid her on the couch because he was getting so aggressive and in my face. When I stood up straight from laying Darla down, he punched me in the stomach and I doubled over. I heard Darla crying, and he kicked me in the head. When I fell on the ground he reached down and grabbed my hair. Then he just started hitting me over and over until I blacked out."

Grace's tremors became violet shakes and tears streamed down both her cheeks. She hadn't worn make up because she knew it was a possibility that when telling her story, she might get emotional. Going over it with Rebecca the night before helped some, but no matter how prepared she thought she was, it still made her feel weak inside.

While listening to her friend tell the story in the setting they were in, with the man who assaulted her mere feet away, Rebecca's blood boiled. She thought of all the things she could do to him. It wouldn't be difficult to have him dealt with and never even get close. Being the one to watch him take his last breath was more appealing. She knew she would have to do something, she just wasn't sure what, yet.

The lawyer asked, "Do you think your daughter witnessed the assault, Mrs. Martinez?"

"I'm sure she did. I heard her crying, so she had woken up. When I gained consciousness, Kevin had moved her out of the room and left me in a pool of my own blood."

"What did you do, Mrs. Martinez? Did you call the police?"

"I went to the bathroom and looked at myself in the mirror."

"What did you see?"

"I had a busted lip and a cut above my left eye. My right cheek was swollen and purple."

"Did you call the police?"

"No. Kevin came in the bathroom and told me I better not think about leaving him. He said that if I ever tried to leave him he would kill me."

"What did you do, Mrs. Martinez?"

"I waited until after he had his way with me and fell asleep, then I got some money I had been collecting and hiding over a couple of years. I left and never looked back. I lived like I was on the run for something I had done wrong. The only thing I did wrong was leaving my daughter. I'm here to fix that today."

After Grace's testimony Kevin contacted Grace's lawyer and gave up his rights to Darla on the terms that they would not prosecute him. He did it to save his skin, but it was clear by the look in his eyes that he wasn't happy about it on the last day of court. Grace filed a restraining order on him and he had no visitation or parental rights to claim. Darla was with the sheriff as requested by Grace's lawyer and had been questioned and counseled by child services due to a few phone calls from Rebecca after hearing Grace's full story the night before. She hadn't told Grace because she wanted it to be a surprise that Darla was there and not being mishandled by one of her ex-husbands friends or family. Most of all, she wanted to see the immediate reaction when Grace would see her daughter for the first time in three years.

65

In the waiting room of the family center, Grace chewed her nails. Rebecca said, "I can see you're nervous. Do you want to talk about it?"

"I haven't seen her since she was two, Rebecca. What if she doesn't remember me?"

"Don't worry, baby. She will be happy you came for her. I have a strong feeling about that."

"What about Kevin? What if he comes after us?"

"We filed a protection order, so he can't be caught within a thousand feet of you. Baby, if he does get close to us he'll have more to worry about than the police anyway. You know I carry. I think you should go to the gun range and learn how to use a firearm. Get your license. You already take self-defense. It's another way to further protect yourself."

"I'll think about it, Rebecca. I just don't know. I have to wrap my mind around it. I've never shot a gun before."

"Interesting. Chloe doesn't want to get her concealed handgun license because she shot an innocent man, and you don't want to because you never shot a gun. You're both being driven by fear. I suggest you work past that and quick. I'm not going to push it any further, though."

The social worker came out of the back holding a little girls hand. A wild look projected from the child's eyes. She scanned the room and spotted Grace. In an instant, she released the social workers hand and ran straight to her mother. Her legs were bird like and a blur. She had her mother's dark complexion and long dark brown hair. Grace hadn't even had the chance to stand before Darla threw herself into her and began to cry. Tears flowed down Grace's cheeks and the reunited girls held each other without a word. Grace knew that Darla could remember what happened that night as soon as she had started running to her. There was a sharp pain in her heart and guilt for leaving her behind. A sick feeling flooded Grace's veins.

Rebecca reached over and smoothed Darla's hair. She said, "It's okay, baby. We've got you now."

66

Back at the hotel, packing their bags, Darla wouldn't leave Grace's side. She was timid and had barely spoken a word since the family center. Grace sat on the bed and patted the place beside herself. Darla climbed up and leaned over to rest her head at Grace's side. Tears threatened Grace's eyes again and she embraced Darla. The young girl was shaking.

Grace said, "I'm sorry I left, Darla. I should have taken you with me."

Darla asked, "Why didn't you, mommy? He was so mean to me."

"Did he hurt you?"

"He slapped me and called me names all the time."

Grace broke down into tears. She said, "I'm so sorry, Darla. I thought I had to leave. I didn't think he would hurt you."

"I don't want to go back, mommy. I don't ever want to be around him again."

Grace squeezed tighter, pulling the tiny child close. She said, "You don't have to, baby. We are going to live a whole new life. No one is going to hurt you now."

While folding clothes, and placing them into her

suitcase, Rebecca listened to the conversation between the mother and young daughter. She felt enraged and acid ran through her, she had to breath deep through her nose to contain her furry. If anyone she'd ever laid eyes on needed to be dealt with, it was this Kevin Austin. His day was coming.

67

When they arrived home with Darla in tow, Chloe was ecstatic. To her surprise, Darla remembered her and Barry. She didn't remember Mila as well, but the child's memory was remarkable and it may have been the trauma she endured directly after her last visit to the Apple household that supercharged the recollections. Rebecca took close notice of how she reacted to everyone. The scar on her left cheek was apparent, and when she saw Barry, she touched the scar on her face.

Chloe said, "He doesn't bite so much anymore, Darla."

Darla smiled with a sadness that never left her eyes. She had the look of a wild and tormented animal. Grace had dressed her in an all pink outfit. Frilly dress and bows on her shoes. She'd bathed her and brushed her hair, but there was something about Darla that set her apart. A hesitation and a look in her eyes as though she were constantly searching, looking for ways to escape the moment. She had a distant and pain-filled gaze that betrayed her worries to everyone she made eye contact with.

Grace said, "Come on, baby. Let's go see mommy's

house. Our house."

Darla took Grace's hand and they walked out the back of the main residence and down the stairs leading to the quaint house by the pool. Rebecca and Chloe watched them as they went, and Chloe sighed. She said, "I can't believe she's really here. It didn't take long. I thought you would be gone for a while or that there would be multiple hearings."

"Some things developed in Grace's story, baby. Her coward ex gave up all his parental rights to avoid prosecution."

"Why did you let him do that? What kind of things came up?"

"Baby, it's not important now. They're safe here and assholes like her ex eventually get what's coming to them. I'll let them tell their story again if they choose to, but I don't want to spread it, or prod them about it. I don't think you should either. What we do now is be the best family we can be and try to accommodate them with whatever they might need. Do you agree?"

Chloe bit her lip. She loved when Rebecca talked about being a family. Chloe said, "Yes, I agree."

"Beautiful."

Rebecca's mind churned. She knew she had work to do. What disturbed her most was that Darla was so small and malnourished. Thoughts and imagination of the horrors the girl must have endured plagued Rebecca's mind. Chloe noticed that Rebecca was in some distant place.

Chloe asked, "What are you thinking, Becca?"

"Baby, I'm thinking what a big asshole that girl's father is."

Mila's voice came from behind them. Mila said, "She so small and adorable. Mommy, can she be my sister?"

Chloe bit her lip when she turned around to face Mila. She said, "I bet she'd like that. Why don't you ask her?"

Mila beamed and ran for the back door. Chloe turned to find Rebecca looking at her curiously. Chloe rolled her eyes. She asked, "What is it, Becca?"

"I like to watch you interact. You know that, baby. I was wondering how Barry feels about the new addition."

"It would be absurd to think that he doesn't like her."

"Baby, I'm not saying that. I saw how she looked at him and touched her cheek. He saw it too. I'm wondering how he will interact with her and how he feels knowing he hurt her. He doesn't show emotion much, but I saw a reaction in him. I don't know if it was remorse."

"He should feel bad. He almost bit the poor girl's cheek off. She's scarred for life. I should make him apologize."

"Interesting. I wouldn't do that. I'd let them develop some kind of bond and maybe suggest it to him later. He was two years old when it happened and so was she. I say let them become friends and see if he makes the right decision. If you force it then it won't mean as much to either of them as it would if it came natural. You know, when someone really cares, it makes all the difference."

Chloe began fidgeting and wringing her hands. Rebecca asked, "What's wrong, baby?"

Chloe said, "Mila is ten now and Barry is almost six.

I think it's time we talked to them about us."

Rebecca said, "Beautiful. I know it makes you nervous, are you sure?"

"I'm sure, Becca. We can't keep going on like we have. I'm tired of sneaking around. I love you and I want to be with you. They should know that."

"You know, we can keep sneaking around."

"I know. I'm just tired of it."

"Okay, baby. We'll sit them down tonight."

68

Candle light flickered in the library, Barry and Mila sat patiently waiting to hear what their mother and Rebecca had to say. Rebecca thought a dimly lit room might be more relaxing for the children. Mila played with her hair and rolled her eyes. She sighed as she began to grow impatient for Rebecca to take her seat from lighting numerous candles. Barry wore a scowl. Before he had been called in for the special family meeting, Noma had offered to read him 'The Angry Alligator', a ritual the two had been doing for many months now. Both children thought that the meeting had something to do with Darla. That was the big event of the day and the reason that Mila was so restless. She had been interrupted from a game of patty cake and she liked teaching Darla how to play.

Rebecca took her seat next to Chloe on the small leather couch facing the two chairs the children were in. Light danced around the room and gave an old-time story telling vibe. Chloe reached over to hold Rebecca's hand. Something she did often and the children were used to seeing. Her palms were sweating and Rebecca squeezed lightly to reassure Chloe.

Chloe looked from Barry to Mila. She asked, "Do you have any idea why we asked you in here?"

The children shook their heads and tension built in the room. Rebecca asked, "How was your day with Darla, Mila?"

Mila perked up, excited to talk about the new family member. She said, "It was great. We've been playing games and Aunt Gracie said she was my cousin. I don't have any other cousins, so I'm happy. A little girl, here, every day, Who'd ah thunk it? It's awesome."

Rebecca said, "Now, Mila. Haven't we discussed your speaking properly? You're going to be a bad influence on your brother and he's been doing so well."

"Sorry, Aunt Becca. I get carried away. Darla says 'who'd ah thunk it', and I thought it was so cute. Adorable."

Rebecca raised an eyebrow. She said, "Interesting. That may be, but she will learn, also. You don't want to encourage uneducated verbal communication. People won't take you as seriously as they should."

"Heck. I know, Aunt Becca. I remember. I'll do better and help her, too."

"Beautiful. I just want you to be treated like a lady. You are a little lady, aren't you?"

"Yes, ma'am."

Chloe said, "Becca, let's talk about what we're here for."

Barry said, "I want Noma to read to me. What are we here for?"

Chloe said, "We want to talk about love."

Barry shifted in his seat and Mila rolled her eyes. Rebecca asked, "Do you love your mother and I?"

Both children agreed that they did. Chloe said, "When two adults love each other they want to be together a lot. Do you know what I mean?"

Mila said, "I do. Like you and Aunt Becca. Y'all are always together."

Rebecca said, "Yes, baby. That's what we want to talk to you about."

Mila furrowed her brow. She asked, "Are y'all going to split up?"

Rebecca and Chloe looked at each other puzzled. Chloe said to Mila, "We're trying to tell you that we're together, Mila. Do you understand?"

Mila rolled her eyes again. She said, "I'm not stupid, Mommy. I know y'all are together."

"I mean we're together like a couple. Like mommy and daddy were together. How does that make you feel?"

"Mommy, I'm telling you I already knew. Can I go back and play with Darla now?"

"Okay, sweetie. You can go play."

Mila ejected herself from her seat and ran from the room. Barry sat still wearing his scowl. Chloe asked, "What do you think, Barry?"

"I think that I want Noma to read the book to me. I don't know why we had to do this."

Rebecca said, "You can tell us if this bothers you. We might get married soon."

"It doesn't bother me. Can I go find Noma?"

Chloe said, "Go ahead, you grump."

When Barry left the room Chloe and Rebecca sat in silence for a moment, then they kissed in the candle light. Rebecca said, "We had nothing to worry about, baby. We can get married now if you want."

Chloe said, "I don't know. You haven't told me what you do when you leave on trips."

"Baby, sometimes I'm just checking on properties. Even when I'm not just checking on properties, I at least check on one or two when I'm in an area where I have them. Does it really matter if I'm committing professional burglary or whatever?"

"To me it does. I need to know."

"Interesting. We aren't ready then, baby. I don't want to talk about everything, yet."

"When, Becca? It's been long enough. I can handle it. Whatever it is. For God's sake…do you kill people?" Chloe emitted a nervous laugh.

Rebecca raised an eyebrow. She asked, "What if it was that? What if I kill people?"

Chloe released Rebecca's hand and began to fidget. She bit her lip and looked at the floor. She said, "I hope it isn't that. I wouldn't know what to think."

"Baby, let's just leave it alone for now. I'll tell you when the time is right."

"Okay, Becca. I trust you. I don't think you would ever hurt any of us. I just don't want to marry someone with secrets."

"Baby, it is okay, and soon enough you will know everything."

69

It felt real. Peter sat in front of Chloe and reached out to her. The life gone from his eyes, but he stood there and the chill in the air sent shivers up Chloe's back, making her shake with fear. His mouth moved but no words escaped his lips. His fingertips were almost touching her, she woke and sat up quickly in the bed gasping for breath. She looked over and Rebecca rolled and watched her. Chloe wiped sweat from her forehead and climbed out of the bed to go to the bathroom.

She stood in front of the mirror, pale and sickened. After turning on the tap and washing her hands and face, she toweled off and went back into the bedroom. Rebecca sat up with her back to the headboard. Concern marked Rebecca's features and Chloe could see the question in her eyes. Climbing back in bed, Chloe snuggled up against Rebecca.

Rebecca asked, "What happened, baby?"

Chloe shuddered. She said, "It was another dream about Peter. He was like a zombie again. They're getting more realistic."

"Baby, you should start going back to the therapist. It seems to be helping Barry and Mila a lot."

"They're children. They need it more than me. I'm an adult, I should be able to handle a few bad dreams."

"You know, it's okay to seek help. It doesn't make you weak."

"It makes me *feel weak*, Becca. I don't like that. I need to be strong."

"Baby, sometimes to be strong we need help and I think this is one of those times. I'll go with you if you want."

Chloe huffed. She said, "I'll go. I don't need you to hold my hand through it. I can do it."

"Beautiful. It's almost six o'clock. Do you want to get up and make a pot of coffee?"

"Yeah. Coffee sounds good."

Chloe likes it when they are the only ones awake in the house. They would have to wake Mila up for school soon. Chloe asked, "Does Grace plan on enrolling Darla in school today?"

Rebecca said, "She wants Darla to be homeschooled with Barry. We're going to sign her up and get her started today or tomorrow."

"Wasn't she in school in Chicago?"

"Baby, her father was the worst kind of deadbeat. He hadn't even let her start school yet. I think he kept her in the house most of the time being abusive. It pisses me off."

"That's horrible. I hope she can catch up."

"She will be able to if we do summer courses. Everything is going to be fine."

Chloe took a sip of her coffee and thought how much

she loved Rebecca and all that she was doing for them. She asked, "How do you do it, Becca? How do you pull everything together and make it all alright?"

"Baby, I'm not even sure. It's my pleasure. Being with you all has given my life purpose and I think that's worth the effort and every penny spent."

70

On the ride to school, Mila asked Rebecca, "Are you going to be my mommy, too? One of my friends at school has two mommies."

"I don't know, baby. You have to ask your mommy. You can keep calling me Aunt Rebecca if you want."

"I'd rather call you mom. Would that be okay?"

"Like I said, baby. You have to ask your mommy. We don't want to hurt her feelings, do we?"

"I don't think it would hurt her feelings. I can call her mommy and you mom. What's wrong with that?"

"I'm not saying there's anything wrong with it. It's just something we have to talk about. Good families talk about everything."

"Well. I'm glad you're going to be my mom because I know you won't try to replace my dad like some man will. I hope you get married soon."

"Interesting. Why is that?"

"Well, you're already like my mom. If you marry my mommy you really will be my mom."

"I have custody over you, baby. I am your mom."

"Okay."

Mila hopped out of the car and when she turned to

shut her door, she said, "I love you. I'll see you after school, Mom."

She shut the door and darted across the school lawn. Rebecca raised an eyebrow and shook her head. The young girl had a rebellious streak after all. Now Rebecca knew she would have to have a talk with Chloe before Mila came home from school. All the complications spiced up her life and she was enjoying it immensely. She only hoped that Chloe would be able to see the humor and beauty in the new development.

71

Back at the house, Chloe and Grace laid out by the pool with an iced down pitcher of strawberry margaritas, soaking in the morning sun. Grace said, "I'm surprised you didn't balk at my idea and heckle me for being an alcoholic."

Chloe lifted her shades and squinted at Grace mischievously. She said, "I'm not such a square, am I?"

Grace laughed and shook her head. She said, "No ma'am. You aren't a square after all. What gives?"

"Nothing really. I mean, I've been having bad dreams and I just want to relax. Does that make sense?"

"Perfectly. You could let me paint your nails."

"Toes and all?"

"You bet."

Chloe lowered her shades and laid back. She said, "Later. Let's finish our booze."

"Sounds like a plan to me. What are your dreams about?"

"Peter. They're always about Peter."

When Rebecca walked in the house, Darla and Barry were going nuts. They were yelling and throwing couch pillows at Noma, running in circles and every which way like they had been supercharged by sugar and caffeine. Noma was egging on the ruckus, throwing pillows and yelling out silly names. Rebecca stood in the entry way for several seconds before anyone noticed. Barry was the first to see her and he just sat on the couch. When Noma saw, she put down the pillow she was about to bop Darla with. Darla noticed, but didn't care either way. She used the pillow she had to assault Barry and yelled one last name. "Chomper!" Then she sat down next to him, close enough so that he scooted over.

Noma said, "We're just having some early morning fun. Getting ready to do some learning." She looked at the children. She said, "Are we ready to learn?"

Barry said, "I am, June bug."

Rebecca asked, "Why are you calling her that?"

"Because, Aunt Becca. She makes a lot of noise."

Noma said, "I don't mind. We were all making up silly names and bopping each other. I just want them to have fun, you know? I think it's real important to have play time. Darla liked it too, didn't you Darla?" Darla nodded her head.

Rebecca said, "Beautiful. I'm glad everyone is getting along well. We have to get Darla enrolled today and get her started in her studies. Where's her mother?"

"Oh, Ms. Grace and Chloe are out by the pool. Do you want me to get them?"

"Baby, I'm perfectly capable. Why don't you all go in the library and sit quietly to read while I sort things out?"

Noma nodded her head. She said, "Yes, ma'am. I'll pick a book. Come on kids." She put her hands out and both children took a hand each.

Rebecca said, "Interesting. How do you do that?"

"Do what, Ms. Rebecca?"

"How do you get them to trust you completely so quickly?"

"Oh, children have very good senses. I guess I'm just good with them because they don't see me as a threat. That's what my momma used to tell me. I don't know if it's true, but that's why I want to be a children's nurse."

"Beautiful. I'll be in the library shortly. I should find you reading a book."

"Oh, you will."

Rebecca headed for the back door and Noma went towards the library with children in tow. Rebecca stopped and peered through the back-door's glass down at the pool. She took in the sight. The contrast of the two women side by side lying in chase lounges next to the wavy blue water. The beautiful crystal clear water always reminded her that Noma was laid every time the damn thing had been cleaned.

Chloe looked extra pale and gorgeous next to Grace. Grace spent almost every bit of her free time sunbathing and the dark-skinned beauty was darker by the month. Chloe had to wear sunscreen, never carrying a tan and Rebecca hoped she was lathered in it now because she would have to deal with the burns and late night pain moans of her lover if not. Rebecca took a deep breath and opened the back door. It was time to confront a new subject.

Before she stepped out the threshold, her cell phone

began ringing. She checked it and could see it was Griffin. She looked down by the pool and could see Grace and Chloe peering in her direction. Rebecca waved and went back inside. She answered her phone.

Griffin said, "I jus' got the message, boss. Where you wanna meet?"

"Meet me at Oddballs in an hour and a half."

"I'll be there."

Chloe walked in from the back door. She asked, "What's up, Becca? Do you want to join us by the pool?"

"I can't right now, baby. I must go somewhere, but I need to talk to you and Grace. Try to get Darla enrolled in the online courses while I'm gone, that's all I need to talk to Grace about is Darla's education, but I have something important to talk to you about. I don't want to get into it now because I don't want to rush the subject. Noma is in the library with the children. If you could get them started on today's lesson. I'll see you later." Rebecca leaned in and gave Chloe a lingering kiss on her puffy lips.

Chloe said, "I want to spend time with you."

"Later, baby. This is important. Trust me."

"I trust you."

"Beautiful."

72

After collecting the paperwork she had compiled, Rebecca left the house in a calm, casual manner. She drove the speed limit, relaxed like she had nowhere to be. Classical music played on the radio and her thoughts were on Chloe. Being honest with her is something that Rebecca wanted and she thought of ways to approach the subject that one of her pastimes was being a contract killer. It wasn't going to be an easy conversation to have.

She pulled up at Oddballs almost a half hour early as she had planned. When she entered the establishment, most of the sparse clientele didn't acknowledge her arrival. She went to a corner booth and laid the manila folder with the paperwork on the seat beside her. When someone new came in the door she watched close and kept a discrete vigil on the whole place. The waitress approached and Rebecca ordered a vodka with a side of soda.

Griffin showed prompt as usual. He took a seat and they made small talk until the waitress made her round. When it was clear of prying ears to speak of the reason for the meeting, Rebecca passed the manila folder and Griffin placed it beside himself.

Griffin asked, "What's the deal, boss?"

Rebecca said, "The subject in the folder needs to be dealt with extreme prejudice. I want him mugged, beaten, stabbed and shot."

Griffin whistled lightly between his gold teeth. He said, "This one really pissed you off."

"Baby, he's a piece of shit. All the details are in the folder and the job pays seventy grand. It must be done right. I want it to look like a botched robbery, but be a punishment and symbol. He must suffer. I want the article to read to my pleasure. Is that understood?"

"Yeah, boss. I hear ya. You don't sweat a thing, you know I can get it done."

"Why would I sweat, Griffin? You don't want to let me down. Do you?"

"I know better than that, boss."

"Beautiful."

73

When Rebecca arrived home, Grace was leaving in the Escalade. She waved and sped off. Inside the house the children sat with Chloe and Noma in the living room. They were learning their lessons for the day. Everything was tranquil. Rebecca fetched herself a juice and took a seat in the living room with everyone else.

Noma said, "You sure do look nice today, Ms. Rebecca. I like flower dresses. They make me feel innocent. I'm not sure why."

Rebecca raised an eyebrow. She said, "Innocent. What a silly concept."

"Oh, I didn't say I was."

"Baby, you couldn't pass that bar if you tried."

Noma twirled a strand of hair in her fingers. She said, "I can look that way, though. You look innocent in that dress. That's all I'm saying."

"Interesting. Do you think I'm innocent?"

"No one is, ma'am."

"I don't know about that, baby. Darla looks innocent to me. I think she probably is."

Darla said, "I'm bad. That's what my daddy said."

Rebecca asked, "What does your daddy know, baby?

He's one of the worst in my book. We're not going to talk about him right now, though. You and Barry finish your lessons and I'm going to take Chloe somewhere with me. Do you mind watching the children on your own, Noma?"

"Oh, no ma'am, I don't mind. I love these two. Where you going?"

"We're going out to eat and then to the mall to get you all something."

Barry asked, "What are you getting us?"

"It's going to be a surprise. I don't know yet."

Barry scowled. He said, "I hate surprises."

Chloe rolled her eyes. She said, "No you don't you grump. You love surprises. You just think you have to know everything."

Darla tried to roll her dark eyes like Chloe. She said, "Grump."

Everyone laughed in amusement. She pouted her lips. She said, "It's not nice to laugh at me."

Rebecca said, "Don't worry, baby. You're adorable." She looked at Chloe. "Are you ready to go, Chloe?"

Chloe complained. She said, "I'm in my yoga pants."

Rebecca smiled. She said, "Baby, those yoga pants look awesome, but you can change if you'd like."

"I'm going to put a dress on. I'll be right back."

Chloe sprung up and headed for their bedroom. Noma said, "You two are awesome. Y'all are so cute. I wish…"

Rebecca put her hand up pausing the onslaught.

Rebecca raised her eyebrow. She said, "Sometimes I

wish I could sew your mouth shut, Noma."

Noma covered her mouth. She said, "That's horrible, Ms. Rebecca."

Chloe returned in a black sun dress with white polka dots. She spun around in her high heels and smiled. She said, "What do you guys think? I bought it last weekend."

Noma said, "It looks good, Chloe. Now I want to put on a dress, too."

Rebecca said, "Anything would be fine, but you look great. Let's hit the road."

Chloe kissed Darla and Barry and headed out the door with Rebecca. When they got in the Lexus, Chloe leaned over and kissed Rebecca. She asked, "Where are we going?"

"Somewhere quiet to talk. I thought you might want to get out of the house for a while."

"You know me well, Becca. I hope we're going to talk about your secret missions. I'm dying to find out what you do…my mind is running wild."

"Baby, we'll talk about that later. We'll listen to music on the way so we don't run out of things to talk about. Pick something."

"Becca, I like mysterious, but you're ridiculous." Chloe leaned forward and turned the radio on, switching it from the classical station to a heavy metal one. She turned the volume up loud and Rebecca shook her head as she put the car in drive.

74

When Rebecca parked behind the Italian restaurant, Chloe turned down the music and smiled. Rebecca watched her for a moment, glad she had the opportunity to be in the gorgeous woman's life. Sunlight through the windshield shown bright on Chloe's pale skin and Rebecca thought she was what an angel was supposed to look like. She reached over and took Chloe's hand. She squeezed it gently.

Rebecca said, "Are you ready for lasagna?"

Chloe laughed. She said, "You know this is my favorite place and that's my favorite dish."

"Baby, I don't know what you see in this place, really."

Chloe rolled her eyes. She said, "The place doesn't have to be five star to be great."

"Beautiful. Let's go order."

Rebecca walked behind Chloe on the way in and she wondered if it was nervousness she felt. It was hard for her to categorize her feelings because she rarely felt anything at all. Being with the children and her new family she felt so many seemingly new sensations, and felt them often. Chloe skipped up to the back entrance and opened it.

Chloe said, "After you." Curtsying and gesturing with her hand.

Rebecca stifled a laugh and they entered the restaurant. After ordering at the counter they found a seat and waited for their food. Chloe's excitement was palpable. Rebecca loved how excited she could get over the smallest things. When the food was placed in front of them Rebecca shifted in her seat.

Rebecca said, "I brought you here to talk about Mila, baby."

Chloe cut into her lasagna and blew on the hot portion of food. She took a bit and moaned. She asked, "Did she do something bad?"

"Baby, we're talking about Mila. I am noticing a rebellious streak in her, but she's done nothing wrong."

"What is it about then?"

"Baby, she wants to start calling me mom."

Chloe frowned. She asked, "What about me? I'm her mom."

"She said you were her mommy and I was her mom. If that makes sense."

"What did you tell her?"

"I didn't tell her she could or she couldn't, Chloe. I told her we had to talk to you about it."

"I don't know how I feel about that, Becca. It could get confusing."

"Interesting. Are you getting jealous?"

Chloe's pale complexion turned red. She looked at her food and huffed. Looking back at Rebecca she smiled. She said, "I don't know why I get this way. We're on the same team."

"I'm glad you're keeping that in mind. I think it's perfectly acceptable for her to call me mom. If that's okay with you."

"I just don't want to be put on the sidelines, Becca. You're so cool and I know they like you more than me. It's kind of hurtful."

"Baby, I don't think they like me more than you. You've just been around longer and I'm new. Eventually they won't need either of us."

"I doubt that, Becca. You are way too cool to just let go. Me, I'm a bore."

"Chloe, I don't appreciate you talking about yourself like that in front of me. To me you are the most interesting and beautiful creature on earth. Don't forget that. Unless my opinion doesn't matter."

Chloe flushed again. She said, "I love you, Becca. The kids can call you mom if they want. It's okay with me."

"Baby, it doesn't matter to me what they call me. I know that you and they are mine and that's all I care about right now. How's the lasagna?"

Chloe raised a forkful. She said, "It's delicious."

75

Lying in Trey's bed, Grace placed her head on his chest and listened to his heart. The heartbeat of another human being was always soothing to her. She was starting to feel deeply for Trey and she wasn't sure how to express that. Being where she was now in life seemed like a fleeting dream just a few short months' past. Everything was moving fast for her, and in the right direction. She hadn't told her new lover about all that she suffered in the past, or what she wanted out of life. It was uncertain to her what she wanted. It would be easy to fool herself into thinking she wanted another serious relationship. That's not what she wanted and the reason she hadn't invited Trey to the house to meet her daughter.

The thought of all the years she had left Darla to suffer at the hands of her abusive ex conjured tears from her eyes. Her breath caught and she tried to stay unnaturally still. Trey noticed her discomfort and smoothed her hair. He put his fingers under her chin and lifted so that he could consider her eyes. In her dark glistening orbs, he could see her pain and she knew that he could. She turned her head and her gaze away.

Trey asked, "Have I done something to upset you?"

Grace bit her nails. She said, "If you had done something to upset me you would know. I'm verbal."

Trey laughed lightly and with caution. He said, "You sure are. Do you want to talk about what's bothering you?"

"Don't get ahead of yourself. I'm just here for the sex, remember? I don't want to go getting too serious."

Trey wiggled from beside her and stood up. He began pulling his pants on. He said, "It's more than that to me. You're my girl."

"I know how you feel, Trey. I just can't commit to titles. I don't want to complicate things.'

"Are you seeing other people? Is that what's going on? Is that why you don't want me coming to your house anymore?"

"No. It has nothing to do with that. Don't be a jerk."

"Well, tell me what it is. Why are you pulling away?"

"I have my daughter back, Trey. I didn't want to talk about it. She's fragile and I don't want to push anyone on her."

"So, letting her meet your boyfriend would be pushing someone on her? That's ridiculous."

"I knew you would act this way, Trey. That's why I didn't tell you."

"Oh, really. So, I guess I'm not shit. Just a stiff dick."

"That's it. You're a jerk is what you are and I'm leaving."

Grace stood and even amid the argument it was hard for Trey not to observe her body and wonder how he ever lucked upon such a fantastic beauty. He walked over to her and took her hand in his. When he looked her in the eyes, her eyes filled with tears. Before saying another word, he leaned in and gave her a soft lingering kiss.

Trey said, "It's okay. You're my girl. Forget about it. I'll meet your daughter when you want me to. I won't push. Just stay a while longer."

"I've got to go. I'll call you."

Grace dressed and left without speaking another word to Trey. In the parking garage, she sobbed. After the tears subsided, she looked in the mirror and shook her head. She knew now what she had been trying so hard to avoid. It was apparent how much she cared and that she was falling for Trey.

76

After the meal, Chloe and Rebecca talked about how Barry was doing and the self-defense classes they were all taking. Chloe said, "Barry made a friend, I think."

Rebecca raised an eyebrow. She said, "Interesting. Who's the friend?"

"A boy his age named Sterling. They seem to be getting along very well."

Rebecca's plan had worked. She'd asked that Barry be paired with Sterling by pulling Trey to the side and having a quick conversation weeks back. She'd hoped that Barry would warm up to Griffin's son and from the sound of it that's what was happening. It would be a door open if they became good friends.

Rebecca said, "Beautiful. I think that you should try to know the boy and welcome him. Maybe invite him and his parents for a barbeque."

"That's a good idea, Becca. I'll see if I can put something together at the next class."

Rebecca finished her meal feeling pleased with herself and with Griffin for suggesting putting the boys together. The dojo was owned by the organization and so far, everything seemed to be falling in place. The whole family would soon be secured under the organization's umbrella. It had to happen with Rebecca's position, and although things were complicated, all the pieces were fitting nicely together.

77

In the car, Chloe knocked on the passenger window of the Lexus. She asked, "Is this car bullet proof?"

"Baby, all my cars are bulletproof."

"Why?"

"It's not important right now."

"I think it is. Why would you need bulletproof cars?"

"It has to do with the business. I told you I'd tell you all about it someday."

"I'm ready to hear about it now."

"Let's not ruin the afternoon."

"That bad. Well, whatever it is I don't think I'll love you any less, if that helps."

When they pulled up to Mila's school, Mila ran to the car with Gabby. Gabby was a quiet girl and rarely spoke unless she was spoken to. Mila jumped up and down clapping. Chloe opened the door and Mila could hardly contain herself.

Mila said, "Gabby's mother wants to talk to y'all! They said she could spend the night this weekend if it was okay with you…please…say yes!"

Chloe rolled her eyes. She asked, "Where's Gabby's mother?"

Mila twirled a strand of her hair and pointed in the direction of Gabby's mother. She was standing next to a white Mazda mini-van. When Chloe looked in her direction, she waved. Chloe said, "Thanks for putting me on the spot, Mila."

Mila pouted. She said, "I want Gabby to see the house."

Chloe huffed and headed in the direction of the mini-van. Mila grabbed Gabby's hand and they walked behind her. Rebecca was amused at the girl's enthusiasm. She watched closely as the small group closed the gap.

When Chloe reached Gabby's mother, they went through the normal hello's and how are you doing. Neither of them had seen each other since the slumber party months back. Chloe was amazed at how youthful Mrs. Lopez looked with her light brown hair waving in the wind, high cheekbones and fair skin. The sunlight flickering in her green eyes made her look sharp.

Mrs. Lopez said, "Please, Mrs. Apple. Call me Sandra."

"Well, you call me Chloe. These two have been making plans, haven't they." Chloe looked down at the children.

Sandra said, "Mila is all Gabby talks about to her brother when she comes home from school. It's Mila this and Mila that."

Chloe laughed. She said, "I didn't know Gabby spoke in complete sentences. She rarely says a word around me."

Sandra smirked. She said, "She's a shy girl."

Gabby spoke up. She said, "I talk."

Chloe said, "I'm sure you do." She looked at Sandra. "If you want to let her stay the night Friday would be fine. We're planning a barbeque on Saturday if I can get some guests, so you'd be welcome to come and leave with her afterwards. Bring the whole family."

Sandra said, "That sounds perfect. I'll be here Friday after school with her overnight bag. She has a pillow and stuffed unicorn she won't sleep without, so you can have her then and give me the address to your home. What time Saturday?"

"We'll be out by the pool having drinks early then spark up the grill around three. So, any time after noon, really. It'll be going on until late probably, so don't get in a rush. Of course, since Gabby will be there you're welcome to show up any time you want."

"That sounds perfect. My husband loves barbeque and we won't miss it."

"Bring a swimsuit."

"I will, Chloe. Believe me, I like to show off this body. Two kids. Can you believe it?" She put her arms out in a check me out motion.

"I'm glad you're confident. I've had two, but surgery made it where I can't wear a dang bikini."

Sandra smirked. She said, "From what I see you look awesome." She looked down at Gabby. "Come on, baby. Let's go get your brother."

They said goodbye and waved. Walking back to the car, Chloe thought how peculiar Sandra was. It was almost as if Sandra had been hitting on her. Chloe wondered what Mila had told her or Gabby about the family.

Inside the Lexus Rebecca waited patiently. She raised an eyebrow and gave Chloe a curious look. Chloe tried to ignore her. Mila said, "I had a great day, Mommy."

Chloe turned in her seat to face the young girl. She asked, "What have you told your friends about us?"

Mila started to twirl her hair around one of her fingers. She said, "Nothing, really. Everyone knows I have two moms."

Chloe asked, "Why would you tell everyone that?"

"It's okay, Mommy. They all think it's cool."

Chloe huffed and rolled her eyes. She said, "That's great, Mila."

Rebecca interjected. She said, "Baby, take it easy. It's not a big deal."

"It is to me, Becca. I invited Gabby's mother to the barbeque this weekend and I think she was hitting on me."

"Interesting. You might just be paranoid, baby."

"We'll see." Chloe sighed. "I guess it's my fault for being so damned attractive." She smirked at Rebecca.

Rebecca shook her head and started the car. She said, "Beautiful. My baby is conceited."

They drove away with a little humor in the air. Mila asked, "Mom? Did you talk to mommy?"

Chloe gasped. She said, "You two conspirators."

78

At the martial arts studio tension filled the air between Grace and Trey. They hadn't talked further about their relationship and Darla. Chloe took an active interest in their affairs and Grace wasn't pleased. She tried to avoid talking to Chloe about it, but persistent inquiries opened conversation in the locker room.

Grace said, "I don't know why it's so hard to understand, Chloe. I'm thinking about breaking up with him."

"You're so good with him, Gracie. Why would you do that? It doesn't make sense."

"It doesn't have to make sense, short stuff. It is what it is, we had a good time and that's about it."

"It was more than that and you know it. Everyone can see you're crazy about each other."

"That's the point. I don't need him complicating my life any more than it is."

"Gracie, some complications are damn good."

"Yeah, but do I really want someone else to turn sour on me? It's just a matter of time."

"Thinking like that is your problem. You're just waiting for something to fuck up. If you live like that, you'll never be happy. I know he makes you happy."

"I have to think about Darla, Chloe. I can't just bring a man into her life unless I know he's going to be a good man, and that he's going to stay."

"Did Trey do something wrong?"

Grace began biting her finger nails. She said, "He's fucking perfect and it pisses me off."

Chloe rolled her eyes and smirked. She said, "Sounds like you should go out there and dump him right now."

"Shut up, Chloe, you're not funny." Grace playfully tossed a towel at her.

When Chloe and Grace emerged from the bathroom, several parents were there picking up children. Chloe hadn't paid close attention to who picked Sterling up before until today. She thought she'd seen an Asian woman there in earlier weeks, but today there was a man. An intimidating man over six feet tall with tattoos covering his arms and possibly his whole body. The way Sterling responded to the man gave Chloe the impression he was a family member.

Chloe walked up and the man stood well over a head taller than her. She was below his chest. Being there in front of him made her feel like a small child. He looked at her with the same type of curious look that Rebecca did so well. Chloe pulled her nerves together and gathered confidence. After all, some of the nicest people were big and tattooed.

Chloe asked, "Are you Sterling's guardian?"

He laughed, a strange, guttural sound. He said, "Dat's one weird way to ask someone if they someone's parent, shawty. I'm his dad."

Calling her 'shawty' made Chloe uncomfortable. She felt slightly offended like he was making fun of her height. It was bad enough feeling like a midget standing in front of him without strange remarks. Chloe reframed her urge to roll her eyes and say something rude. She thought that his wife must get annoyed often.

She said, "I'm Chloe Apple and your son is friends with my son. I was wondering if you and your family might want to come to our house for a barbeque this weekend."

"It'd jus' be me and my boy. He ain't got no momma."

"What about the lady I see here sometimes?"

"She jus' a help. His momma passed with that cancer."

Chloe felt horrible for some of the things she had been thinking and could feel her face flush. She asked, "What's your name?" She put out her hand.

He reached out and his large mitten of a hand enveloped hers. He said, "I'm Griffin Smith."

When he smiled, he revealed that all his teeth were covered in gold and diamonds. Chloe thought that it was very possible she'd just invited a drug dealer over. After exchanging information, Chloe went out the building where Grace and Barry waited in the Escalade. She climbed in the vehicle and Grace smirked at her.

Grace asked, "Who was that?"

"Don't start, Gracie. It was Barry's friend's father. They're coming over this weekend for the barbeque."

Barry said, "I'm hungry."

Chloe rolled her eyes. She said, "You're always hungry, mister."

Grace said, "Put the headphones on, Barry. We'll turn a movie on so you don't think about being hungry until we get home."

Barry groaned and put the headphones on. Grace pushed the DVD button and a cartoon came on the truck's monitors. Grace looked in the mirror to make sure that his attention was on the movie. She said, "I talked to Trey, short stuff."

Chloe beamed and bit her lip. She asked, "What happened?"

"I invited him to the barbeque. I told him to act like we weren't together. I mean, he can talk to me there, but no butt grabbing. I said that if Darla likes him without thinking she has to that we could be together."

Chloe smirked and rolled her eyes. She said, "You're a weird one, Gracie."

"Aren't we all?"

79

When they arrived home, they found Mila and Rebecca along with Darla and Noma completing their self-defense practice. Chloe's mind wandered to Rebecca's bulletproofing of all the vehicles. She'd practically forbidden Chloe to drive her old—and unarmored—Toyota. With all the martial arts training for everyone in the house and Rebecca's mysterious rendezvous and trips where she couldn't be reached for days, Chloe suspected that whatever Rebecca's secret was it had to be a dark one.

Rebecca walked up to Chloe and kissed her. She asked, "How was class?"

"It was good. I talked to Sterling's father. He's a strange one."

Rebecca knew all too well just how strange Griffin was. She fanned her hand in front of her face and fluttered her eyes. She said, "Whatever do you mean, baby? All men are strange."

"Wait till you see this guy. He's like seven feet tall and covered in tattoos. His whole mouth is full of gold and diamonds."

"Sounds like a big thug. I'm sure you're exaggerating

his height, though."

"Well, I don't know if he's seven feet, but he's freakin' tall."

"You know, he could be a decent person."

"I know. I'm trying not to judge him by his appearance. You would grit your teeth if you talked to him. He speaks…never mind."

"Baby, just say it."

"Ghetto. Alright. Now I feel like a judgmental bitch. Thanks."

Rebecca laughed. She said, "Baby, some people *are* ghetto. It's just a simple fact. No need to feel bad for recognizing the obvious. At least we have the chance to hook Barry up with a friend he can spend time with his own age. A boy. So, if his father is a little ghetto, so what." Rebecca asked her next question already knowing the answer. "Is the mother coming?"

"Becca, I felt so bad when I asked about Sterling's mother, she died of cancer. I feel horrible."

Chloe tried to read Rebecca in that moment and registered nothing. Rebecca said, "Let's get inside with everyone else and get a snack. You must be hungry after your workout. Life can be sad, can't it, baby?"

"Yes."

"Okay, we won't dwell on that."

After entering the house and eating tuna sandwiches that Grace busily prepared, Rebecca retired to the room to make a phone call. Griffin answered in a few short rings. Rebecca said, "Interesting. Your wife died of cancer?"

"What tha fuck did ya want me to tell 'er?"

"You could have simply said she disappeared."

"Yeah. She prolly wouldn't a blushed so red."

"Don't make me regret making this connection."

"Shit, boss. I couldn't tell 'er my wife's in a unmarked grave fo' tryin' ta go to tha police. Could I?"

"Just do what you know. We don't tell lies that don't ring true if we can help it. You know that."

"Boss. It did. If she fines out bout she disappeared, I'll say I tell everyone that because it's easier to explain."

"Don't fuck this up, Griffin. I will fucking castrate you."

"Yes, ma'am. I got you."

"I need you to watch her, not scare her. So, don't start with all the wanting to get your dick wet shit either."

"Boss, I got you. No sweat."

Griffin knew she meant business and that she would kill him or have him killed as quickly as she had his wife. He wasn't cross about the situation, he had presented the problem and known how it had to be dealt with. He also knew that Rebecca could be the most ruthless agent in the organization. No one wanted to be on her bad side.

80

Friday came quickly and Mila was excited to have Gabby in the car with them. She introduced Rebecca as 'Becca', and Gabby showed a little excitement for the weekend and getting to spend time with her friend. She said, "Thank you for having me, Ms. Becca. Do you really live in a mansion?"

"Baby, I wouldn't call it a mansion. Buckle up your seat belts and let's roll."

At the same time in Chicago, Illinois, Kevin Austin collected his paycheck from the temporary service he'd been working for. After leaving the office of the staffing agency he headed straight for the small convenience store where he normally cashed his check, utterly unaware he was being observed and had been for several days. Kevin didn't own a car and his apartment building stood just a few blocks away. When he would leave the store with his money for the day he would head the same direction routinely to go home and call his dealer for an insatiable crack habit.

Unaware of the danger lurking to lure him into a trap, he left the store with his meager pay in pocket and a bottle of cheap wine. It was one of those days that gave

Chicago its famous subtitle, 'the windy city'. A gust of wind blew his old tattered and faded, puke-green ball cap off and sent it tumbling ahead.

Two men stood well-dressed by the alleyway and one stooped and retrieved the stray article right about the time Kevin picked up his pace to catch the piece of his shabby wardrobe. The man dusted the hat off as Kevin approached. The man held the ballcap out and Kevin took it warily. They were biggish guys and although finely dressed they both looked tough and weathered.

Kevin said, "Thanks."

The biggest of the two said, "It's nothing, buddy. Hey, you wouldn't be interested in scoring a little dope, would you?"

The smaller guy flashed a hand full of 'crack', which was nothing more than little chunks of solid baking soda with some coloration to give it a yellow tint. Kevin, oblivious to the ruse, had the fever. When he saw what he thought could be a potential high, the men could read the desire on his face.

Kevin shook his head. He said, "I don't know, man. I've never seen you two around here before."

The big guy said, "Hey, buddy, what the fuck are you tryin' to say? You callin' us cops?'

Kevin's fear became palpable. He said, "No, man. I don't mean to offend. I'm just saying."

The smaller guy laughed. He said, "I tell you what. I don't like doing business out in the open because the fuckin' cops. Step back here in the alley and I'll give you double your money and my number for when you need some more. Just because you haven't seen us around don't mean we aren't."

The prospect of getting double his money made Kevin's mouth water. Dealing with guys like these might keep him high longer. Those chunks looked fat to him as it was. He took the bait and walked into the alleyway with the two men, behind the convenience store dumpster. His senses became heightened that he was in trouble right about the time the biggest of the two grabbed him from behind and pulled his arms back like a schoolyard bully. The smaller man hit him so hard in the stomach, he began gagging and lost his lunch. When he looked up with eyes watering he felt horrified to see the stocky tough donning a pair of well-worn brass knuckles.

The thug grabbed Kevin by the hair and before Kevin could get out a yell for help, the man hit him in the throat. The situation escalated quickly when in methodical succession the stocky goon hit him in the nose and the mouth. Kevin coughed up loose teeth and the assailant laughed.

The brass knuckle wielding goon asked his partner, "Do you think that's enough?"

"You know the orders. Fuck it, give 'em one more."

The stocky man drew back and nailed Kevin right below the eye, breaking his socket. Kevin's eyeball dangled freely. The stalky man said, "Alright, now we're talkin'."

He put away his brass knuckles and pulled out a long sharp blade, stabbing Kevin in the gut three times. The bigger goon let the battered man fall to the ground. He pulled out a .40 caliber pistol. They didn't care about the noise. That was part of the deal. They took Kevin's cheap bottle of wine, his wallet and his cheap watch along with all the loose bills they could get from his pockets. He positioned Kevin's head to face the concrete. After dropping the fake crack next to him, the smaller man nodded to the bigger man. The single shot to the back of Kevin's skull made pulp of what was left of his face.

The two men walked out of the opposite end of the alleyway like they hadn't a care in the world and climbed into a stolen car, driving away composed, but swiftly. Having heard the gunshot inside the convenience store, the clerk called the police and Kevin's body was discovered shortly afterward. The detectives on the scene tried to sort out the mess. It looked like a robbery and drug deal gone sour. They would later determine that Kevin was trying to sell fake goods on a local gang's turf after finding cocaine in Kevin's system.

81

Late Friday night, Grace came into the main house to talk to Rebecca and Chloe. The girls were in Mila's room playing quietly and Grace had a bewildered look when she sat in the master bedroom with Rebecca and Chloe. Her eyes were filled with tears and worry emanated from her.

Grace began to whisper. She said, "Kevin's dead. His cousin called me. She said they're having his funeral on Monday and they want to know if I can bring Darla. He's gonna have a closed casket. Someone murdered him and destroyed his face."

Rebecca said, "Baby, you don't have to whisper. This room has been sound proofed way before we moved in. Maybe you should ask Darla if she wants to go. If she does, I'll take her. Unless you want to."

Grace bit her fingernail and shook her head. She said, "I don't want to go. Don't I have to?"

Chloe said, "Of course not, sweetie. You don't have to go and neither does Darla."

"I have to ask her though, right? I mean, I'd be wrong if I didn't."

"Baby, after all that man put both of you through,

neither of you have to feel bad if you don't want to go to his funeral. I know some of the things he did and I say good riddance."

Grace groaned. She said, "That's how I want to be. Shit. First Samuel and now this jerk. I don't know what's going on. All my ex's are getting killed and both behind drugs. This is something to do with gangs and drugs. What's next?"

Rebecca said, "Baby, don't worry yourself too much. They were both into some shit they shouldn't have been. These things happen. Do you want me to talk to Darla for you?"

"No. I can do it."

Grace went into Mila's room and asked Darla to come out so she could talk to her. Darla looked downcast like she feared she was in trouble. Grace brought her down the hall to sit in a plush chair that sat under a window looking over the manicured front lawn and fountain. Grace knelt in front of the fragile girl and brushed a piece of stray hair out of Darla's face, tucking it behind her ear. She could see the concern on the poor child's face.

Grace asked, "What's going through your mind?"

Darla pulled the strand of hair loose and twirled it around her finger. She asked, "Am I in trouble? I didn't mean to be loud."

"No. Honey, you're not in trouble. I have something important to talk to you about. I don't want you to be upset, but this might make you upset."

"What is it?"

"Honey, your dad is dead."

Darla showed no emotion. Grace touched her cheek. She said, "You can cry if you want."

"I don't want to cry, Mommy. I hated him. I'm sorry."

"No, no, honey. Don't be sorry. Do you want to go to his funeral?"

"No."

"Okay. You can go back and play if you want."

"I just wanna sit here. I don't want to play right now."

"Are you sure you're okay?"

"I'm okay."

"Do you want me to sit here with you?"

"No. I want to sit alone and think for a while, Mommy. I'm okay."

Grace left Darla alone, reluctantly. When she was out of sight, a wide smile spread on Darla's face and tears filled her eyes. Darla had harbored a fear that her father would come in the night and steal her. She had lived with that fear in the guest house every night since she had been saved from the monster that her father had been.

Barry's door opened slowly and he poked his head out. Barry said, "I'm sorry about your father."

"You heard?"

"My door was open for the hall light. I was staring at the wall thinking about my poppa when y'all started talking. I didn't mean to hear."

Darla hopped down from the chair and put her finger to her mouth signaling Barry to be quiet. She went into his room and took his hand leading him to the bed. She hopped up on the mattress and patted the space next to her for Barry.

When Barry climbed up, she touched the scar on her face. She asked, "Do you remember when you did this?"

Barry furrowed his brow. He said, "No."

"I do. I remember everything. I even remember some things from when I was in the crib. I remember everything."

"If you're trying to make me feel bad, it's not working."

"Well, whether you feel bad or not, you owe me. So, I'm gonna tell you some things and you have to promise me you won't ever tell no one."

"What kinds of things?"

"It doesn't matter. You have to promise to keep my secrets. All of them and always."

"Do I have to?"

"Yes."

"Okay. I promise."

"No. You have to touch my scar when you say it." Darla pouted her lips.

Barry groaned. He said, "I don't want to touch your scar."

"You have to."

Barry reached up and touched Darla's cheek. He said "I promise to keep your secrets."

"Okay. I'll tell you, but you remember that you always have to keep my secrets."

"I got it, I got it. Jeez."

A dark look came upon Darla and she spoke as if she was the only one in the room. She said, "I remember everything. My dad used to beat me for any little thing and I couldn't make a peep without making him mad. He used to make me so hungry. He wouldn't feed me for a long time and I remember every time he starved me. Worst of all, he touched me." A tear streaked down Darla's face. She said, "He touched me a lot and I remember. I want to forget so bad that I want to die sometimes. I remember everything."

Barry didn't know what to say. He opened his mouth but couldn't form any words. Darla said, "I'm glad he's dead. I hope he died horrible. I wouldn't go to his funeral if they tried to make me. He told me he'd kill me if I ever told. I'm free now."

She looked at Barry with eyes brimming and overflowing with pain. He felt frozen in the moment. Her words, and the way she said them, touched something deep within him, filling his chest with her agony. He reached over and took her hand and she squeezed his fingers.

Barry said, "I'll never tell anyone any of your secrets ever, Darla." He reached up and touched her cheek. He said, "I promise."

82

At noon Saturday, Griffin arrived with Sterling in tow. They were the first to show and Barry became excited to see his friend and on a strange occurrence to the adults, Darla tagged along with the boys. She stayed close to Barry and tried to do everything the boys did. Chloe mused that Darla must have a crush on Barry.

Rebecca raised her eyebrow and watched Chloe observe the children. She said, "It's not so strange, you know. Little girls pick the most stubborn boys sometimes. Don't you agree?"

"It's surprising, though. Barry scarred her for life and now they're buddies. It doesn't make much sense."

The doorbell rang and when Noma answered there stood Stephen Mink. Almost six feet tall with light caramel skin glowing, in swim trunks, flip flops and a tank top holding a foil covered bowl. Chloe took at his muscular build and abruptly looked away. She hadn't seen Stephen since the night at the dance club with Rebecca. She knew he was Rebecca's lover and a pang of jealousy formed in her gut.

When he entered, he walked straight up to Rebecca and lifted the bowl slightly. He winked and smiled. He said, "I brought the potato salad."

Rebecca held out her hand and he kissed her knuckles. The sight infuriated Chloe and her insides rolled over. When he turned to her he took her hand and kissed it, too. Butterflies aroused in Chloe's stomach then and she felt ridiculous, like a girl on the schoolyard. Her emotions were conflicting and she wondered what Rebecca must be thinking to invite a former lover to their home.

Stephen walked away and immediately started a rapport with Griffin. Chloe casually wondered which of the two men might win in a tussle. She turned to Rebecca with question in her eyes. Rebecca said, "I'll explain later, baby. Stephen is going to work the grill and later tonight we'll all have a talk. Let's get one of those margaritas and go lay out by the pool. The children are having a wonderful time out there. Aren't they?"

Chloe looked down by the pool and watched Mila and Gabby splash each other. She rolled her eyes and huffed. She said, "Fine, Becca. Let's drink and have a good time."

The next guests to arrive were the rest of the Lopez family. There was an unusual height difference between Mr. and Mrs. Lopez. Sandra was a full head taller than her portly husband. When Mr. Lopez went to the grill to talk to the men and drink beer, his height looked even further out of place beside the giants.

Chloe observed the men interacting closely and her eyes kept locking on Stephen. Rebecca knew where Chloe was looking and it amused her. The sun shone bright and in the warm weather, Rebecca could see that Chloe's nipples were hard. It wasn't hard to imagine that

Chloe was thinking of Rebecca and the hunk of a man entangled. Rebecca licked her lips.

She said, "Baby, I think tonight I'll tell you some things you've been dying to know. If you don't mind, Stephen will be there with us."

Chloe looked at Rebecca and bit her lip. She asked, "Have you been sleeping with him since we've been together?"

"No, baby. I wouldn't do that without talking to you."

"Is he mixed with something? His skin is dark, but his hair is straight. He looks like a super tan white guy, but I'm thinking he's mixed."

"We're all mixed with something. Aren't we? Does it bother you?"

Chloe smirked. She said, "Why would it bother me, Becca? I don't care. I was just wondering."

Rebecca raised her eyebrow. She said, "Baby, you're always wondering, aren't you? He has Indian blood, but he's mostly white."

Chloe rolled her eyes and laughed. She said, "You love my curiosity. That's what you say. What kind of Indian? Dot or feather?"

"Interesting. You like that now. Curiosity. Feather."

Chloe bit her lip. She said, "I thought he was part black."

"I know. He looks that way. Are we done talking about Stephen?"

Sandra walked over to where Chloe and Rebecca were sun bathing and made herself comfortable in the chase lounge next to Chloe. She fanned herself in her small white and pink polka dotted number. She asked, "Are either of those guys yours?"

Chloe smirked and shook her head. Sandra said, "Good. Which one of them was checking out my ass on the way over here?"

Rebecca said, "Your husband."

"That doesn't surprise me. He's always eyeballing me. What were you girls talking about?"

Rebecca leaned forward and lifted her shades to peer at Sandra. She said, "We were just talking about your ass. Isn't that funny?"

Sandra waved her off. She said, "Oh, stop. You're just flattering me now."

Barry, Sterling and Darla came running out of the house together and the boys were in the lead. Barry was yelling, "Don't let her catch you, man! She's got cooties!"

Darla's little skinny legs were a blur as she did her best to catch and tag one of the boys. Chloe smiled to herself. They really were a family and it made her feel peaceful inside. The whole scene was a pleasure. She noticed all the men's attention going to the back of the property. Chloe turned to see Grace emerging from the guest house in a blue string bikini. The kind of ensemble that was almost inappropriate for the children, but it covered all the necessary parts.

Sandra said, "My God. You girls keep a golden goddess in the pool house. I know who Carlos will be eyeballing now."

Chloe said, "That's Grace. She lives here. Darla is her daughter."

Grace sat down in the chase lounge next to Sandra. She said, "Lady, I'm more worried about you than the men over there."

Sandra said, "Don't be silly. I don't bite. I'm Sandra." Sandra put out her hand and Grace reached out and squeezed it lightly.

Grace said, "I'm Grace."

"So I've been told."

"Great." She leaned forward and stared at Chloe and Rebecca. She asked, "Have you two birds been talking about me?"

Rebecca laughed. She said, "We were just telling Sandra that we keep a golden goddess in the guest house."

"How freakin' kind. We ought to have a swimsuit contest. There's three judges here."

Chloe bit her lip. She said, "I don't know about that."

Sandra said, "Oh, look. Another judge just arrived with the young girl from the door."

Noma and Trey laughed together as they walked down the steps to the poolside. Noma walked up to Rebecca and said, "This lug caught me dancing and now he says I looked like I was having a seizure." She punched Trey in the arm.

Trey said, "Alright, dang. No need to get violent."

Rebecca said, "I like the trunks and shirt, Trey. Touristy."

Trey said, "I actually got these threads in Hawaii. I guess they're my favorites. So, how are you gorgeous ladies doing? Can I get you some more drinks? I'll be that guy today."

Grace said, "Honey, you better be that guy every day. I could use one."

"Coming right up. Anyone else?"

Sandra said, "I'll take one, sugar." She made a point to bat her eyelashes.

Trey went inside to refill Sandra's margarita and get Grace a fresh one. When he was out of ear shot, Sandra turned to Chloe. She asked, "How about that one? What's his story?"

Chloe said, "I'm pretty sure he's spoken for."

Grace growled. She said, "He is. Aren't you here with your husband?"

"That slob. He's so bad in the sack."

Chloe put her hand on Sandra's arm. She said, "That's enough, Sandra…why don't we just enjoy the day. You can pick up guys when your husband isn't yards away."

Mila and Gabby sat on the steps of the pool halfway submerged in the water watching the older women interact. Gabby said, "Do you see how my mom looks at those guys. She's such a slut."

Mila gasped. She said, "Don't say stuff like that."

"It's true. Sometimes on the way home from school we go by a man's house. I can hear them in the room. Even over his stupid T.V."

Mila didn't know what to say to her friend, so she splashed her and the pool war continued.

83

When most of the company left and the children had passed out from a full day of play, Rebecca brought Stephen and Chloe into the master bedroom to talk in private. There were two sitting chairs on either side of a small table in the room and Rebecca asked that Stephen and Chloe take a seat.

Rebecca said, "I have you both here so that you can be clear of your roles. Chloe, Stephen is my sub. He only sleeps with me and the penalty for sleeping with anyone else without my express permission is much worse than a spanking. It is punishable by death if I so choose."

Chloe rolled her eyes and laughed. She said, "Stop fooling around, Becca."

"Baby, I'm not joking. Am I Stephen?"

"No, boss."

Chloe shook her head. She said, "This is too cute, but I'm not buying. I mean, it's fun and could be exciting, but the whole boss thing is too much."

Rebecca looked in her eyes. She said, "Did you think you would have a dickless marriage to me? Stephen is my dick. I'm going to tell you what you have been dying to hear tonight. I must warn you that you will be obligated to silence about the subjects I will reveal." She looked at Stephen. She said, "Stand up."

Stephen did as he was told and Rebecca crossed the room and grabbed his crotch. She smirked at Chloe and raised her eyebrow. She asked, "Do you want to see it, Chloe?"

"I don't know, Becca. This is a little weird to me."

"If you want, we can call everything off. I'll leave the house now, with Stephen and give you the house, an allowance and properties to do with as you please, some in this very neighborhood. Or you can join me in all my deviance and perversions. The choice is yours, but choose quick."

Chloe bit her lip. She said, "Let me see it."

Rebecca unbuckled and unzipped Stephen's pants and pulled out a large throbbing member. Chloe looked at Stephen and he winked at her. When Rebecca started stroking his rod it grew in length and girth. Then she did a come here motion with her finger asking Chloe to approach. When Chloe stood, her legs shook.

When she stood directly in front of Stephen, Chloe could see how big his cock was and it scared her. Rebecca said, "Get on your knees, Chloe."

Chloe did as she was told. When Rebecca instructed her to take Stephen in her mouth she did and Rebecca began to pace slowly behind her. Rebecca said, "You keep sucking, baby. I'm about to tell you a story, and don't you stop. I'm going to start from some time in the beginning of the organization that I now run for this region of Texas and the organization spans most of the globe. We are something like the C.I.A., but nothing like it. Chloe, Stephen doesn't call me boss because he's my sub. He calls me boss because I am the boss. We do many things and one of those things is assassination."

Chloe stopped what she was doing and attempted to look back. Before she could fix her eyes on Rebecca, Rebecca put her hand on the back of Chloe's head. Rebecca spoke coldly and with authority. She said, "Keep. Sucking. His. Dick."

Chloe placed her mouth back on Stephen's rod and Rebecca continued. She said, "My father's father founded the organization many decades ago, along with a group of highly trained and organized men. It grew and today our numbers are staggering. More than that, we work with numerous groups. We deal in the black market and have our hands in just about everything. I'm not going to name the organization. That wouldn't be prudent. I am telling you these things so that you know not to question me, ever, in public or in detail. You will have only the information I choose to share. Anything I tell you will be expected to be kept confidential. I will protect you and we are now in a bond for life. You must understand that I do love you. I want only the best for you. Do you believe me?"

Chloe nodded her head slightly, never neglecting her task. Rebecca said, "Beautiful. Stephen, pick Chloe up and put her on the bed. Undress her and fuck her while I watch."

To Chloe the situation felt surreal. Rebecca on the sidelines and Stephen obeying her every order. She let go and pleasure flooded her veins, like a narcotic inhibiting her ability to think straight. The feel of the moment seemed something like what Chloe imagined making a pornographic movie might feel. It had been so long since she had sex that Chloe couldn't help but to close her eyes and imagine Peter. Chloe stiffened up.

She said, "Stop."

Stephen seized all motion, still buried inside of Chloe's most intimate spot. Rebecca asked, "What's wrong, baby?"

Chloe said, "It's been so long. I like it, it's just."

"Go ahead, baby. Say what you're thinking."

"I keep having images of Peter pop in my head. Could I try again later?"

Stephen pulled out of Chloe's vagina. Rebecca said, "Baby, you can try again any time you want. Stephen is my dick, so he's yours now, also. I'm going to store his number in your phone. You call him whenever you want. I'll have him back for both of us soon. As a matter of fact, you shouldn't leave him wanting, it's not fair."

Rebecca began to undress herself and she climbed in bed next to Chloe. She said, "Come on, Steph. Let's show Chloe how it's done."

While watching Rebecca and Stephen, Chloe began to become more aroused then when she was having sex herself. A feeling of shame rose inside of her. She thought what kind of person she must be becoming. Even with her shameful feelings, she didn't take her eyes away from her lovers. When the debauchery came to an end, Chloe watched Stephen get dressed and wondered to herself how life had taken such a turn for her that she was now in a love triangle.

Stephen exited through the doors to the veranda. Chloe wondered if the sole reason Rebecca bought a house with the master bedroom downstairs was for this very thing. When Stephen had been gone a while, Rebecca asked Chloe to lay down in the bed with her. Chloe crossed the room and when she laid her head on the pillow, Rebecca stroked Chloe's long soft hair.

Rebecca said, "I love your blonde hair. It makes me jealous."

Chloe laughed lightly. She said, "You don't get jealous, Becca."

"Baby, I do. A worse kind of jealousy than mere envy. I want to talk to you about it. If you ever cheated on me, I don't know what I might do."

"Kill me?"

"No. I don't think I could do that. But you can be sure that I would be livid. I don't want you to sleep with anyone but me and Stephen. Ever."

"I won't, Becca."

"Do you have any questions for me, Chloe?"

"When can I…well, when can I call Stephen. If I want."

"Whenever you want."

"I'm sore."

"Let's take a bubble bath, then we can sleep."

Rebecca felt pleased that Chloe didn't want to quiz her about the organization. It made her feel comfortable with what she shared. Only time would reveal Chloe's character fully, but from what Rebecca knew, she was loyal. Loyalty and dependability, in Rebecca's mind, were the most important characteristics of a person. It was the main reason why she didn't kill Grace. Something she didn't want to explain to the woman who would soon be her wife.

84

Under the impression that her life would get increasingly unusual, Chloe popped a Xanax pill in her mouth and returned to the bedroom. Rebecca had left to take care of whatever business she had to conduct on a Sunday morning and the morning sun barley peeked through the opening in the thick drapes that covered the door to the veranda. The veranda. Memories of the night before flooded Chloe's mind and an urge rose to call Stephen and have another session. Just thinking of calling him made her feel guilty. Peter wouldn't be coming back, but she couldn't force herself to let go and really live.

When she left her room still dressed in her silk nightgown, she found Noma making a pot of coffee. Noma asked, "How was the rest of the barbecue yesterday? I had a good time with James. I know it isn't going anywhere, but he's fun. I'm young anyway. No need to settle down. Oh, I saw a man leaving when I came home late last night. Do you know who he was? Handsome guy, with dark hair and kind of a caramel complexion. He looked like the guy from the barbecue. The one working the grill. I'm not sure. He used the side gate, so I figured you or Ms. Becca gave him the code. Weird, though, he went walking up the street. When he saw me he smiled and winked at me. His teeth were really white in the dark. He didn't seem startled when he saw me looking or anything. I didn't think much of it, but it was really late. I didn't want to knock and disturb you. I just checked on the kids and went to bed. I hope that's okay."

Chloe said, "Noma. You're talking way too fast for so early in the morning."

"Oh, I'm sorry. I have a lot of energy in the mornings, you know. So, who was that guy?"

"Don't worry about it. Don't mention it to the children or Grace and please, don't ask a bunch of questions. He's just a friend of mine and Rebecca's. That's all you need to know."

"Oh, okay. I'm sorry. I thought it would be good to mention it. Just in case. I didn't mean to aggravate you. I—"

Chloe put her hand up—a signal that Noma had become accustomed to. Chloe said, "Sweetie, you're just too much in the morning. Please, let me get a cup of coffee in me."

"Oh, yes ma'am. I'm sorry."

85

The smell of bacon, eggs and toast filled the air. Chloe sipped on her second cup of coffee while Noma served the children. Grace sat at the end of the table gazing off as though she might be considering the motions of the galaxy. Darla sat right next to Barry and he smiled his checkered grin when she looked his way. Observing the anomaly, Chloe's curiosity swelled.

Chloe asked, "What are you two up to? Why are you smiling so much, Barry?"

Barry furrowed his brow and took a bite of eggs. Darla said, "We're friends. Aren't we, Barry?"

Mila laughed. She said, "Boo-boo never smiles. I didn't see."

Chloe said, "He smiled alright."

Grace came back to reality in the middle of the ongoing conversation as quickly as if she'd been sleeping and was suddenly doused with water. She said, "Chloe, leave the poor babies alone. They can be friends."

Chloe rolled her eyes. She said, "Welcome to the land of the living, Gracie. I thought we were losing you there, but apparently, you follow conversations while you're in la-la land." Mila and Darla laughed.

Noma sat at the table, and when the kids finished and headed off to the living room to watch cartoons, Chloe smirked at Grace. She said, "I bet I can guess what's in your mind."

Noma said, "I know what's on her mind. Her man. Did you do it last night? I did it with James like four times. That's why I didn't come home until the wee hours. His thing isn't all that big, but he knows how to work it and he lasts a long time. Have you guys ever had someone like that? You know. Small junk but he knew how to use it? It doesn't bother me too much because my stuff is kind of, well, I'm not deep."

Chloe said, "Noma, you are deplorable."

"I'm just making conversation. I know I can't be the only one who got laid."

Chloe flushed, but refused to talk about her experience. Her business would be kept quiet as long as she could help it. She knew that Noma had a pretty good idea what Stephen was doing before he left out that side gate and she knew the young woman was fishing. Grace broke the awkward pause with a sigh.

She said, "I would have liked to see Trey last night, but I didn't invite him. I guess I just wanted to think about the day. He hardly said a word to Darla. I wonder if he liked her. All he did was play with the boys. Big and small. Darla was right there with the boys and he didn't show her much attention.

Noma said, "Maybe he thought it would be weird to show her too much attention. Some guys are like that. They don't show the little girls too much attention. You know what I mean? It's like they don't know how to interact with them very well. Maybe they just know boy stuff?"

Grace said, "He teaches little girls in his class. I don't think that's what it is. I'm just going to have to talk to him."

Chloe said, "At least you're not breaking up with him over it."

"I might."

"Sweetie, don't do that. He's a good one."

"I know. I just want someone who will accept Darla. That's not asking too much, is it?"

Noma twirled a thick strand of hair around her pointer finger. She said, "I don't think it's too much to ask, but a good man is hard to find. I'd have to think about it. I bet if he got around Darla more he wouldn't be such a stiff with her."

Grace peered into nowhere then shook her head. She said, "I'm being too critical. You girls are right. I'm going to talk to him. I'll be back."

Chloe looked startled. She asked, "You're leaving right now?"

"You bet. Well, I'm gonna shower first and get ready." She started biting her fingernail. She asked, "Do you think he still wants to see me?"

Chloe rolled her eyes. She said, "Sweetie, he would be a worthless fool if he didn't."

86

After inspecting the newly armored BMW 6 series coupe, Rebecca paid the custom shop and made arrangements for its delivery. With all the options and a V8 motor, the beast of a car would be perfect in her mind. All that was left to do would be to go home and wait for its arrival. Pleased with her selection and herself, Rebecca drove home smiling and contented.

When she arrived home, she waited out front of the house until the delivery was made and called inside to Chloe. Chloe said, "I wasn't expecting you back so soon. Let me get some clothes on and I'll be right out."

Rebecca stood next to the car and when Chloe came out, she looked over the shiny white vehicle with big matching chrome and white wheels. A bow hung from the driver's side mirror. Chloe asked, "Is this what I think it is?"

Rebecca raised an eyebrow. She said, "I hope you like it because I can't take it back."

Chloe went to Rebecca and embraced her. She said, "It looks perfect. Can I get out of this robe and take it for a drive?"

"Baby, you can do whatever you want. It's yours."

Chloe smirked. She said, "Stephen's in the room."

Rebecca laughed. She asked, "So soon? You tramp." She winked. "I thought you were sore."

"I am, Becca. I just couldn't give up that easy. You're not mad, are you?"

"Not at all, baby. I told you to call him. Remember? Let's go in and do whatever, then we go for a drive. Okay?"

"I want to get dressed and drive."

"Baby, it's your call. Do I have to finish for you again? You know that's going to get old. It's not cool to leave a man hanging."

Chloe bit her lip. She said, "I don't mind getting him off. He already did twice."

Rebecca gasped. She said, "You are a tramp. Baby, I'm not sure what I started, but pace yourself."

Chloe rolled her eyes. She said, "This is coming from someone who 'showed me how it is done' for hours last night. I almost dozed off."

"It didn't look like you were dozing to me, baby. He's a lot more fun than a power tool, though. Isn't he?"

"And I'm the tramp." Chloe rolled her eyes.

87

At Trey's apartment, Grace made herself comfortable on his couch and Trey rubbed her feet. Grace said, "You hardly said two words to Darla at the barbecue yesterday. I saw you near her, playing with the boys, but you didn't really play with her. What's gives?"

"Babe, you know you're my girl. I want your daughter to like me, she's just shy. It was like she was scared of me or something. Has she been hurt by someone?"

"Honey, her father was a real jerk."

"I can kick his ass if you want."

"Simmer down, he's dead."

"Dang, I'm sorry. How'd he die?"

"It doesn't really matter. He was a jerk and I'm glad he's gone. He's probably the reason Darla acts like she does with men. Scratch that, I know he's the reason."

"So, you want to do something...you know."

Grace twirled a strand of hair around her finger. She asked, "Are you trying to take advantage of me?"

Trey leaned in to kiss her and they spent the rest of the afternoon *enjoying* each other's company.

88

When Chloe pushed the pedal of her new BMW to the floor, the car shot forward making the other cars traveling the highway a blur. She felt exhilarated. After letting off the gas she turned to Rebecca and smirked. She asked, "I'm not complaining, but why the coupe?"

"Baby, I figured you always had mom-mobiles and I wanted you to have something nice."

Chloe reached up and opened the sunroof. She said, "You did good. This is nice. Is it bulletproof?"

"You know, you shouldn't have to ask me that, but yes."

"I feel important in it."

"You are important, baby."

Chloe smiled and accelerated again. When they pulled up to the house, Mila and Noma were out front. They had bags from the mall. Mila walked to the car smiling. Rebecca rolled down the window and Mila held her bag up.

Mila said, "Noma bought me stuffed animals."

Noma approached. She said, "Thanks again for giving me the Camry. It drives so good. This is a nice car. It's definitely an upgrade. I got some new shorts at the mall.

Are y'all hungry? We were about to eat. I can make enough for all of us."

Rebecca said, "You girls go ahead. We're going to sit in the car and talk for a while."

Noma and Mila went inside and Rebecca turned to Chloe. She said, "Beautiful. It looks like everyone is happy. You know. You said we could get married if I told you everything. Well, now you know everything. Will you marry me?" Rebecca produced a moderately sized, but gorgeous ring.

Chloe bit her lip. She twirled her wedding ring from her last marriage around her finger and then started fidgeting. Her thoughts passed to Peter and all the years of marriage and ups and downs, his death. She thought of the life Rebecca led and the life that was unfolding in front of her. Rebecca's eyes were unwavering. Chloe pulled her ring off.

She said, "I'll marry you, Becca." She held out her hand and Rebecca slid on the new wedding ring."

Rebecca said, "I've got something in the trunk for you, baby."

Chloe popped the trunk and she looked inside. A cherry wood jewelry box sat in the center. Tears filled Chloe's eyes. She opened the box and a diamond pendant necklace sparkled brilliantly. Rebecca said, "I thought we could start a new collection for you."

Chloe turned to Rebecca and hugged her. She went straight inside and put her old ring in her old jewelry box and placed the box in top of the large walk-in closet. Rebecca put Chloe's new box on the vanity and a new day dawned. Pleased with Chloe's willingness to move forward, Rebecca gave her a long and lingering kiss.

89

Grace pulled on her pants and stood in her bra with her hands on her hips. She said, "I don't know what we're doing here."

Trey said, "I have a good idea what we're doing."

He went and kneeled in front of her. He asked, "Will you marry me, Grace?"

Grace flushed when he produced a diamond ring. She said, "Yes."

Trey slipped the ring on her finger and Grace looked at it closer. She asked, "Where the heck were you hiding this rock?"

Trey laughed. He said, "Up my butt."

Grace slapped him on the shoulder. She said, "You're not funny, jerk."

Trey stood and embraced her. They considered each other's eyes and Grace's fears about him began to melt away. She said, "Don't ever hurt me."

Trey said, "You're my girl. I'm going to protect you." He kissed her hard and fast. Off came Grace's pants and bra.

90

During the summer both couples were married and Trey moved into the guest house with Grace until they could find a place. Barry went to the door of the guest house each morning to ask if Darla could play. Grace thought it was cute that Barry and Darla practiced karate together and with Trey there, they were learning fast. Trey would often get in the back yard with the children and play fight. Grace liked to sun bathe and watch the action.

Being happy and contented didn't seem like something that could be achieved again to Chloe after Peter's death, but looking out of the back-door's glass at the scene in the yard made Chloe feel content. She didn't want to dwell on the past and although the dreams didn't cease to haunt her in the night, she found that she thought about the day Peter was murdered less during her waking hours. The change of pace and new developments in her own and Grace's lives made the days easier to bear.

Mila approached Chloe at the back door. She said, "Mommy. I'm going with mom to buy a new dress. Do you want to come?"

Chloe reached and smoothed Mila's hair. She said, "You go ahead, sweetie. Mommy wants to relax."

Everything seemed just right and things were going smooth. Rebecca had been taking Grace to the auctions and helping her invest in real estate. Chloe had what seemed like an unlimited amount of funds at her disposal and life had become sweet and somewhat simple with all her basic needs met. Though she didn't think of Peter's death often in her waking hours, she did think of Peter and wondered if he was watching over her, and if he was, what must he be thinking?

The whole family, including Noma, who had become an integral part of the family, sat at the large oak dining table that night for dinner. Chloe had started cooking every night so that everyone sat together in one place for a short time in the evening. Barry and Darla sat together and Mila stayed attached at Rebecca's hip with Noma by Mila's other side. Mila liked to dance, and she and Noma did a lot of it. Trey and Grace were inseparable, and Stephen joined them each evening for dinner. He no longer had to sneak through the back of the house. Although they didn't discuss the nature of Stephen's visits or relationship to Chloe and Rebecca, it had become an unspoken apparent. Strange as it may be, the entire household had accepted Stephen as their own and no one seemed to mind that they were all the odd family on the block.

After dinner and during dessert, Barry struck up conversation. He said, "I want to go to a big school."

Chloe rolled her eyes. She said, "I don't know about

that, mister."

Darla said, "I want to go to a big school, too. I want to go with Barry."

Grace said, "Honey, you can go to school at a big one if you want, but I don't think Barry can."

Barry looked at Rebecca and furrowed his brow. He said, "You told me if I was good and learned all my lessons I could go to a big school. I've been good."

"You know. You're right. I did say that. I think it's up to your momma now. I don't have a problem with it."

Chloe huffed. She said, "Great. I've got to be the bad guy."

Rebecca raised her eyebrow. She said, "Baby, you don't have to be the bad guy."

Chloe bit her lip. She said, "I really don't want to be." She looked at Barry with a smirk. She asked, "Do you think you're ready to go to school and behave, for real this time?"

Barry said, "I can be good. I know I can."

Chloe relented. She said, "Okay. You can go to regular school this year."

Darla lit up and looked to her mother. She said, "Ohh, Momma, can I go to school with Barry? I've never been."

Grace bit her fingernail then abruptly dropped her hand from her mouth. She said, "Yes. You can go."

Darla jumped from her seat and hugged her mom. She grabbed Barry's hand and the two ran off to the living room together. Grace shook her head. She said, "They didn't excuse themselves." She looked to Trey. "Do you think that's a bad sign?"

Trey laughed. He said, "They're just excited, babe. Kids. I'm sure they'll be fine."

Stephen cleared his throat. He said, "This cheesecake is delicious, Chloe. You did a good job."

Noma said, "I think we need to dance the cheesecake off." She looked at Mila and smiled.

Rebecca laughed. She said, "Beautiful. Wine and dancing should break the tension."

91

Rebecca went to the market alone late in the morning to pick up some random groceries that Chloe wanted for the evening meal. She didn't mind shopping for Chloe and the line was short. When she noticed Griffin in the checkout line a few rows over, she didn't think much of the fact that he was buying condoms and whipped cream. Her cashier checked her out at about the same time as Griffin and she approached him by his car. The person sitting in his car who he no doubt bought the whipped cream and condoms for was no other that Gabby's mother, Sandra. The look on Sandra's face was priceless.

Rebecca raised her eyebrow and stared at Griffin. She said, "You know you're asking for trouble with this one."

"I'm jus' getting' my dick wet, boss."

"Don't call me that. She might hear you."

"I'm sorry, Rebecca. What do you want me to say? I'ma dog an' you know it. She been beggin' me for it since the barbecue."

"That was a while back. How long have you been fucking her?"

"Well, since the barbecue."

"She's Mila's friend's mother, Griffin. Don't get

caught up with this woman. I'm telling you that she's trouble."

"Look. I'll be careful. I have been. We won't get caught."

"It's messy, Griffin. Real close to my home. Do you want to upset me?"

"No, bo—, Rebecca. You know I don't wanna do dat. It ain't serious."

"I forbid it to go past this day. Break it off."

Griffin climbed in his car with Sandra and drove away. Rebecca had the feeling that it wasn't over. She could see disaster heading her way behind the confrontation and she didn't like the feeling of uncertainty. Sandra was the type of person that could cause a major disruption.

92

Rebecca went home and found Chloe in the garage, shining the wheels of the BMW. Chloe smiled and waved until she noticed Rebecca's demeanor. After Rebecca exited the Lexus, Chloe approached her and gave her a kiss. She stepped back and considered her lover's eyes.

Chloe asked, "What's eating you?"

"It's nothing, baby. People at grocery stores piss me off sometimes. Why are you shining your wheels? We have that done."

"I like to do it myself sometimes. They get dusty before the car gets washed."

"Interesting. You barely drive it. How would they get dusty?"

Chloe feigned offense. She said, "I drive it. Her name is Candy because she's so sweet. Did you forget?"

Rebecca raised an eyebrow. She said, "You rub Candy more than you drive her."

Chloe laughed. She said, "I just want to keep her fresh and new."

"Beautiful. Help me bring in the groceries and let's check on the girls."

Inside the main house music played loudly and they

found Noma, Mila and Gabby all dancing around singing. Chloe went to the wall mounted home theater controls and turned the music down significantly. The young girls protested and Mila sat on the couch to pout. Darla was missing from the party as usual.

Chloe asked, "Where did Darla go?"

Noma said, "She ran off with Barry to play cars. I swear that girl is a tomboy. She even got overalls to match him today. I guess if her mother doesn't see anything wrong with it I shouldn't. I mean, there's nothing wrong with it."

Mila said, "Can we turn the music back up? I was having fun."

Rebecca shook her head. She said, "This place is turning into a mad house."

The doorbell rang and Rebecca turned on the porch monitor. Sandra stood displayed on the big screen television. Noma went to open the door and Rebecca thought that whatever the aggravated looking woman was going to have to say was likely to be interesting. Sandra walked in and asked to speak to Rebecca alone. Chloe began to protest, but Rebecca agreed to have the private discussion with the irate women.

They went to the library and shut the door. Rebecca crossed the room to the built-in liquor cabinet and poured herself a brandy. She offered one to Sandra and the rude woman waved her off without a word. Rebecca ignored the woman's insolence and took a seat in one of the two arm chairs in the room gesturing to the other. Sandra curled her lip and continued to stand. Calm and collected, Rebecca took a sip of brandy and raised an eyebrow at Sandra.

Rebecca asked, "Did you come here to talk, or to stare at me, crossly, all afternoon?"

Sandra started tapping her foot. She said, "You were talking to Griffin this afternoon. What did you say to him?"

"That's really not your concern. I simply told him he could do better than a married woman, if you must know."

"Are you sleeping with him?"

Rebecca laughed. She said, "That's genuine. I detect a hint of jealousy in your voice."

"Just tell me so I can move on. You must be sleeping with him because when we left the store he broke it off with me."

"Interesting. The cheater wants to know if her secret lover is 'cheating.' No. I'm not sleeping with Griffin."

Sandra put her hands on her hips and cocked her head to the side. The expression on her face was one of hatred. She said, "I'll fuck you up if I find out he's sleeping with you."

Rebecca sat her glass on the table next to the chair. She stood erect and pointed to the library doors. She said, "I think it's time you made your exit."

Sandra said, "You think I'm playing?" She reached out and pushed Rebecca's shoulder.

Without giving it a thought and in a swift and fluid motion, Rebecca chopped Sandra in the throat. The aggravation that marked Sandra's face turned to fear and panic as she clutched her throat and tried to breath. She fell to her knees and Rebecca sat back down in her chair. She lifted her glass of brandy and took a sip before Sandra could gain her abilities to swallow a lung full of air. Sandra started panting.

Rebecca said, "I suggest you take a seat and gain your bearings."

Sandra crawled onto the couch and caught her breath. The tension in the room thickened and Rebecca finished her glass. She stood for a refill and Sandra flinched like she could be attacked at any moment. Rebecca filled her glass and filled one for Sandra. She crossed the room and handed the glass to the wounded woman. Sandra sat up and took a small sip.

Rebecca sat and smirked. She said, "Don't walk into another woman's home and make threats. I'm not sure how you were raised, but I'm not some little bitch you can push around. If you want to talk to me, keep it civil. You don't want me to get ugly."

Sandra rubbed her throat. She said, "You don't understand. I can't stand my husband. I don't get laid often and he's horrible in bed."

Rebecca raised her eyebrow. She said, "If it's that bad, get a divorce."

"I don't want a divorce. What would I do? I don't work."

"Interesting. You feel like you need your husband, but you can't stand him."

"Perfect. I already feel silly without you judging me."

"Baby, don't give me that shit. We all judge each

other."

"I look good. I feel trapped. Like I'm going to be with this hideous man all my good years and then I'll be stuck when my looks fade. I don't want to be a cheater. You have to understand, I'm in a loveless marriage."

"Interesting. I don't think Griffin is that interested in you. Maybe you should get up the nerve to divorce and find someone you really want to be with."

"Could you help me?"

"I don't know about that."

"What about Chloe? Would you let her help me? I know y'all helped Grace. I talk to the girls a lot when Mila's at my house. She said you helped Grace. I need help."

Rebecca shifted in her seat. She said, "That's not what we're all about. Grace is special to Chloe and Chloe is special to me. It was duty for both of us."

"But you did help her. You even got her a career."

Rebecca stared at Sandra in contemplation. She said, "Mila likes to talk, doesn't she? We should talk to Chloe. If she agrees to help you so will I."

Sandra's eyes filled with tears. She said, "Thank you, Rebecca."

93

Rebecca called Chloe into the room after instructing Sandra to listen to what she had to say before speaking. The women sat down in the chairs with Sandra on the couch. Rebecca said, "Sandra came here today seeking help, Chloe. What do you think about that?"

"She wasn't acting like she needed help when she came in."

Rebecca laughed. She said, "Sandra has some emotional problems she's going to have to learn how to deal with better if she's going to be around us."

Chloe rolled her eyes. She asked, "What is all this nonsense about? You know I have a patience problem."

"Baby, Sandra feels stuck in a loveless marriage and she wants to know if we will help her out of it."

"I don't know." Chloe turned to look Sandra in the eyes. She said, "You've been unpleasantly abrasive."

Sandra said, "I can be better. If you help me I'll do whatever you say."

Rebecca looked at Chloe and raised her eyebrow. She said, "How about it, Chloe? Putty in your hands. Your very own project, baby."

Chloe rolled her eyes. She asked, "Is that really what

I need? A project?"

"Baby, you spend all your time in this house and don't even drive your new car. Maybe this will help you as much as it helps her."

Rebecca looked at Sandra. She said, "Not that I approve of the condition of your proposed project now."

Sandra said, "I can get better. I really can."

Rebecca spoke in a threatening tone. She said, "If you hit on my wife or make her uncomfortable I'll make your life hell."

Sandra's fear and tension filled the room. She said, "I wouldn't. I won't do anything to cross you."

Chloe said, "We'll help you."

94

Grace and Trey moved things from the guest home to their new three-bedroom place a few blocks away. The day was warm but comfortable. When the move was over Grace laid out by the pool in her bikini and Trey went into the main house to drink a cold beer on the living room couch. Rebecca wandered in and sat in the arm chair. She watched Trey and grinned.

He asked, "What is it, boss?"

Rebecca said, "I didn't expect this development. When I sent Grace to you I wanted you to train her. What happened exactly?"

"We fell for each other. I tried to stand off. I'm glad I didn't."

"Have you told her anything about the organization?"

"Why would I, boss. I'm just a hand to hand combat trainer. I don't need to explain how the rent gets paid or that most of my clients are being trained for the field. It doesn't matter. I don't do wet work."

"No. You don't. There's no need to go into details about your employers. I don't want her to know I'm your boss."

"She won't. I know how to keep things discrete."

"Beautiful. Treat her right."

"Is that an order?"

"Let's say your life depends on it."

95

When the new school year began, Noma drove to Darla's home with Barry and they picked her up. A few miles up the road Noma dropped the children off and wished them a good day. Barry held Darla's hand and they found their first class together. The teacher welcomed students to sit down after entering the classroom and Barry and Darla found a place to sit together. Rowdy children filled the room and Barry felt anxious.

Darla hadn't been around so many children before. She said, "I don't know if I like this, Barry. It's not like I thought."

Barry said, "It's okay. I'm with you."

They smiled their checkered grins at one another. At the same time, Mila was starting at the private school. She had a desk behind Gabby. The two girls had been spending a lot of time together and Gabby was happier because her mother hadn't been cheating on her father for a few months. At least not that she knew because her mother didn't bring her to sit on strange guy's couches. Her demeanor was different this morning, though. Mila noticed that she seemed sad.

Mila asked, "Is everything okay, Gabby?"

Gabby pouted her lips. She said, "My mother asked my dad for a divorce."

Mila didn't know what to say, so she left the subject alone. She said, "We had a great summer, huh?"

"It was, but now there's this. I don't understand why they have to do this to me. If they get a divorce I know I'll have to go with my mom. I love my dad. He's so funny, and he would do anything for me."

"I'm sure your mom loves you."

"She's irresponsible. She always brought me places to cheat on my father and I don't think it's right. I shouldn't have to lie and hide things from my dad for her."

The bell rang and the rest of the class started taking their seats.

96

Barry and Darla's class split into groups to do crafts. They were making macaroni face pictures. A boy next to Darla took an interest in her and squirted glue on her paper. She furrowed her brow at the boy and moved closer to Barry. The spectacle made Barry angry, but he stayed calm and helped Darla make her macaroni face. They laughed at the silly pictures they made and forgot about the boy to the other side of Darla.

After lunch their class took recess. Barry and Darla played by the monkey bars. Darla twirled in her blue flower dress and laughed. Barry sat watching, amused. The boy from class approached and pushed Darla. Barry bolted at the boy yelling.

He said, "Don't touch her!"

Without thought he used the high kick he had learned from Trey and it landed at the boy's chest, knocking him to the ground. Their teacher observed the attack and rushed over to quell any further violence. Barry was sent to the principal's office while the other boy cried and was tended to.

Rebecca received the call about Barry's assault while she sat next to Chloe in the car. There was no way to talk in private and Chloe overheard everything. Worse, they were close to the school and the principal was asking that Barry be picked up.

Chloe asked, "What did he do exactly, Becca?"

"Baby, he just got in a fight. Boys fight."

"That's how it all started. I don't know why we agreed to let him go back to public school. This is his first day. He doesn't know how to behave."

"Let's pick him up and let him explain himself, baby."

Frustration built inside Chloe and she felt like she might burst. When they arrived at the school, Rebecca went inside and did all the talking. She came out leading Barry by the hand. He wore a scowl and Chloe fumed about his insolence. The ride home was quiet and Chloe held her frustration and questions inside, knowing that if she did start to express herself she wouldn't be able to stop herself from saying things that would be irreversibly damaging.

At the house, Chloe's mood didn't improve. She grabbed Barry by the shirt as soon as they walked in the door and dragged him up the stairs and into the room. He hit his bedroom floor with a thud. She felt possessed when she slapped him. Blow after blow, Barry didn't cry out, but he balled up. Chloe kicked him.

She said, "This is how you got your father killed you little shit!"

Rebecca entered the room and put her hand on Chloe's shoulder. She said, "That's enough, baby. This isn't helping."

Chloe turned to Rebecca and put her head on her

shoulder. She sobbed and breathed heavily, wretchedly. Rebecca said, "Let's go to the room and cool down."

Chloe left the room and Rebecca knelt by Barry's side. She rubbed his back and smoothed his hair. She asked, "Are you okay, Barry?"

Barry stood and wiped the silent tears from his eyes. He said, "I was just protecting Darla, Mom. I don't want you to die, too."

"No one is going to kill me today, baby. You stay here and I'll be back after I talk to your momma."

Rebecca went to the master bedroom and found that Chloe had locked herself in the bathroom. Rebecca tapped on the door and listened. She could hear Chloe crying. She said, "Open up, baby. We can talk about it."

Chloe's voice was shaky when she answered. She said, "I don't want to talk. Just leave me be."

Reluctantly, Rebecca walked away to let Chloe have some space. She went to the kitchen where she found Noma. She said, "Pour us some wine, baby. All of a sudden my nerves are bad."

97

Chloe stared at herself in the mirror. She had never hit her children and the way she attacked Barry made her feel like a monster. Her blue eyes filled with tears and she sat on the toilet lid with her face in her hands. What was she becoming? How could she have let herself lose control completely? The questions swirled in her mind and made her body shake with anxiety.

She went to the pill cabinet and retrieved the full bottle of Xanax she kept for when she had extreme anxiety. Opening the lid, she looked in the bottle at the little blue football shaped pills and then poured out a couple into her palm. After filling a glass with water, she swallowed the pills. Thinking of the day Peter was shot and how much she blamed Barry. She wished it could all go away.

Chloe began dumping pills in her hand and swallowing them. It didn't take long before she had the whole bottle down. She leaned against the counter and sobbed. Then she went to the bathtub and filled it with water. Before the tub was halfway full, Chloe faded to blackness and slumped on the floor.

Rebecca heard the bathtub running and knocked

again. Chloe didn't answer and the hairs on Rebecca's arms stood. Rebecca said, "Baby, are you alright?"

No answer. Rebecca said, "Say something to me, baby. If you don't, I'm coming in."

With no response, Rebecca acted quickly. She went to her safe in the walk-in closet and retrieved her lock picks. It didn't take long to get in. She saw Chloe mumbling softly, delirious and sprawled out on the floor, a quick glance at the counter and the empty bottle along with the used glass told her all she needed to know. She pulled Chloe's head up and began to try to make her vomit up whatever she could get out of her. She yelled for Noma and it wasn't long before the young girl came rushing into the bathroom.

Rebecca said, "Call an ambulance."

98

The ambulance rocked and swayed on the way to the hospital. Rebecca held Chloe's hand while the paramedics performed various activities. Things were bad and Rebecca knew it. There would be questions about Chloe's competence to be married to someone so high in the dangerous organization that Rebecca had been born into. She knew why Chloe did what she did, with all the commotion that rang in time with what happened with Peter. It had sent her over the edge. Although to Rebecca grief wasn't an acceptable excuse to attempt suicide, she understood. The question was whether her peers would be able to overlook this moment of weakness.

Chloe mumbled almost inaudibly. She said, "The pink ones. The. The pink ones."

It made no sense and whatever world she resided in at the moment had to be subversive and strange. When the ambulance came to a stop at the hospital, Chloe was wheeled into Emergency Services and Rebecca went to the waiting room. She knew she should call Griffin since he was the overseer for the relationship. Everything would be reported through him about the household status. Everyone was appointed an overseer in the organization. Although Rebecca's word held greater weight in most matters, Griffin's held weight in these types of matters. There would be a meeting that Rebecca would not be present for by the statute of the organization.

It wasn't hard to imagine that things could get messy quick. Rebecca pulled her phone out to make the call, then she heard someone walking up to her. It was Griffin. He did his job well and for that Rebecca would always be proud, with the exception that this time the issue was the woman she loved.

Griffin said, "Can I get you anything, boss?"

"I don't need anything, Griffin. You work fast."

"I always do, boss. You know that."

"This isn't a potential threat. She has her reasons for doing what she did and they have nothing to do with us."

"Dat might be so, boss. You know I have to talk to her if she makes it."

Rebecca said, "She tried to overdose on Xanax. It's difficult to commit suicide with that and she hadn't been drinking."

"Boss. You can only commit suicide when captured. It's frowned on. Dis shit could be bad, but if you let me talk to her first, I'll do wat I can to make dis shit blow over."

Rebecca thought about when she executed Griffin's wife. It was a different type of situation and everyone knew it had to be done, even him. She couldn't help not thinking that somewhere deep down, Griffin was sour about her fate. Rebecca placed her phone in her purse and smirked.

She said, "Griffin, this isn't a threat. I would appreciate your support."

"Is dat right? You gon' let me hit that fine ass?"

"Interesting. Always a dog, even in the worst situations."

"So, is dat a yes or no?"

"You'll hit the pavement before you hit this and you know it. Stop being an ass and tell me. Will you support me?"

"Boss, if she ain't a threat, I got your back."

"Beautiful."

99

The whole family—Noma, Grace, Trey, and children—were at the hospital within the hour. Everyone looked downcast and as the night drew on, the doctor came out to the waiting room to let everyone know that Chloe would be fine, but that she was sleeping, and when she woke she could have visitors. Rebecca directed Noma to bring the children home and for Grace and Trey to come back in the morning if they wished to. Only Griffin and Rebecca stayed.

When it came time for a visit, Griffin went first, by himself. Rebecca didn't often feel anxiety, but the situation resonated anxiety inside her. Watching Griffin go back to Chloe's private room was like watching death approach the place a loved one dwelled and not being able to do anything about it. She tried calming techniques and took a seat quietly awaiting a verdict.

Griffin entered the dimly lit room and could see Chloe's eyes flutter at his entrance. Griffin asked, "Are you awake, Chloe?"

Chloe's eyes fluttered again and he could see she was straining to comprehend who it was at her bedside. Griffin said, "It's Griffin, Chloe. Can I talk to ya a minute? It'll be quick." Griffin thought he would make her death painless if it came to that.

Chloe slurred, "Griffin? What are you doing here?"

"Rebecca wanted me to talk to you. She's shook up. She wants to know why you did this."

"She knows. It's that bastard, Barry. He got his father killed and he just won't stop. I didn't mean to hit him, Griffin." Tears started rolling down her cheeks.

She said, "I'm a bad, bad mom. I wish I didn't wake up."

"You don' mean that, Chloe."

"I love my children, and Rebecca. I'm just no good."

"Woman. You are the only person in the world that believes you ain't no good. Let me go talk to Rebecca and she gon' come back here an get wit chu. I'll see you later."

Griffin left the room and approached Rebecca. He could see the question in her eyes. He said, "It's cool, boss. I'll call the meeting. Everything'll be alright. She needs some confidence, boss. You should talk wit 'er."

Rebecca's heart lightened although she knew she would be the last to hear if the decision didn't go her way and that if it went south, there would be nothing she could do to save Chloe. The whirlwind in her mind quieted when she walked into Chloe's room and laid eyes on her. Her lover looked frail and vulnerable in the bed that seemed to swallow her. Her appearance pale and her tiny hands on her stomach. Chloe looked at Rebecca and broke down into a wretched sob.

After taking a seat beside the bed, Rebecca reached over and put her hand out for Chloe to hold. Chloe calmed and found it hard to look Rebecca in the eyes. The shame she felt inside ate at her very core. She had tried to take the coward's way out and the feeling of regret constricted tightly in her chest, so intense that she felt suffocated and bewildered. Attempting suicide went against her beliefs. All the thoughts she had of it and fought off after Peter's death were now her failed reality.

Rebecca said, "Baby, I'm glad you're still with me. I don't think I've ever felt as helpless as when I thought you could die. For some reason, I thought that we were unbreakable."

"I'm not unbreakable, Becca. I'm broken, and you are going to try to fix me, I know, but I can't be fixed."

"What are you saying, Chloe?"

"I'm saying that I'm damaged and that I'm no good."

"Baby, that's not true. Sometimes we do things we aren't proud of. It's human to be desperate. It's human to feel dismal. We have to work past that."

"I don't know if I can. Everyone's going to know, Becca. No one will look at me the same. No one will treat me the same."

"That's not true, Chloe. I will. I love you."

"I know you do. I love you, too. Why would you want to be with me after this?"

"Because, baby. You're my wife and I know you. You know me. We both know why this happened and we're going to work things out."

"I don't want to take care of Barry anymore. I wish we could send him away."

"Baby, we aren't sending him anywhere. You let me

take care of Barry and you don't have to worry about him. He's mine and he'll stay that way for the rest of his life. I love the children the same as I love you."

"Why are you so good to me, Becca?" Tears rolled down Chloe's pale cheeks. She said, "I don't understand."

"Baby, you don't have to understand why someone that loves you is good to you. Sometimes it can't be explained. Besides, you haven't come close to doing anything that would make me turn my back on you. I don't know how the others will feel about what you've done, but my feelings for you haven't changed. You have to believe that, Chloe."

Chloe bit her lip and considered Rebecca's eyes. Rebecca could see the pain in Chloe's, the embarrassment. Rebecca searched for words to secure her lover. She started to speak, and Chloe looked away. A nurse walked in doing rounds and left.

Chloe said, "I want to go home."

Rebecca shifted in her seat. She said, "You're going to be admitted to the psychiatric ward for observation and diagnosis. They think you have chronic depression given the direction your life has gone. Either way, I think it needs to be done."

Chloe looked Rebecca in the eyes. She said, "I'm not crazy."

"No one's saying that, baby. We just need to make sure that if you need help you get it."

"How long will I be there?"

"I'm not sure. It might not be long. I want you to promise me that you will be open about the things you are feeling with the doctors."

"I will."

"Another thing, baby. Something I don't feel like I should have to say. Don't mention our secrets."

"I'll never do that. I wouldn't, Becca."

"Beautiful."

Darla and Mila showed up in the doorway and Rebecca waved them in.

100

When Rebecca left the hospital, she knew that if the verdict went bad there would be a chain of unstoppable events. She tried to guess how it would go down. To clear her mind, she turned the radio up high with loud classical music vibrating through the speakers. The worst part about the situation was that she had no control over Chloe's fate. Even worse, it could snowball significantly.

Her cell phone rang. She looked at the caller ID and could see it was Sandra. Rebecca answered reluctantly. She asked, "What is it?"

Sandra said, "I'm supposed to move today and Chloe said she would be here with a guy so I didn't have to move alone with my husband. He gets weird and I don't want to go to the house alone."

"Baby, Chloe's going to be unavailable for a few days. I'll send someone to meet you."

Rebecca hung up the phone and called Stephen. She said, "Just get over there and help keep her husband from freaking out on her. I'll give you the number for the movers and she's going to one of my complexes. The one over in East Fort Worth. Gable Gardens. You know the place and I already gave her the keys and everything.

She can be a little loose and I want a full report when the job is done."

"You got it, boss."

Rebecca had given her an apartment owned by the organization. Sandra didn't know that the living room smoke detector was a camera. Rebecca felt comfortable about helping her as long as she could be watched. The woman had potential to be a headache and trouble, so she didn't trust her. Hopefully Sandra wouldn't find out about Chloe, but since her daughter was Mila's best friend, keeping it under wraps was less likely. The apartment made it accessible for Gabby to continue private school with Mila.

Rebecca called Sandra back. She said, "My guy should be calling you."

"He did. He's on his way. Thanks."

"Beautiful."

"Rebecca? I just wanted to say thanks for the place and agreeing to pay for Gabby's school, getting me a job. Everything."

"You know, it's important that you understand. You do not want to piss me off."

"I wouldn't do anything to upset you."

"Beautiful. I'm a private person…if you violate that…I'll cut you off."

"I won't. I only have good things to say about you and Chloe."

"Let's keep it that way, baby."

"I just want everything to be perfect. I don't want to jeopardize that."

"Another thing. The man that's coming to meet you. He's hands off. Understand?"

"If you say so. Hands off."

"Interesting. I do say so."

"I'm not gonna mess this up."

"Don't."

Rebecca ended the phone call with Sandra and cleared her mind. She turned her music up again and pressed the accelerator to the floor entering the highway.

101

Barry was home with Noma when Rebecca arrived. He looked downcast and it would be difficult to explain to him that despite everything that his mother did, it wasn't his fault. He knew the stress he caused her and that was enough to set in his mind that he was the reason. Noma went about her chores and left Rebecca and Barry alone in the living room.

Rebecca sat next to Barry and rustled his head. She said, "You look like you didn't get much sleep last night."

"Is my momma gonna be okay?"

Rebecca raised her eyebrow. She said, "Is she *going to* be okay? I don't know. It's hard to tell for certain. Why don't you let me worry about your momma? What do you think about going to the ice cream parlor? Just you and me?"

"I don't know. I don't deserve ice cream."

"Sure, you do. We have something to talk about. I think it would be a great place to go have a conversation. What do you say?"

Barry said, "Okay." In a hushed tone.

There was no talking on the way to the ice cream parlor. Bach played softly over the car stereo speakers and the late morning shadows danced through the tree limbs and off the car giving a calming strobe-like effect as they drove through the neighborhood. Rebecca wondered what must be going through Barry's head. He was calm and for someone who had indirectly killed his father and drove his mother to suicide, he held his composure well.

After parking in front of the ice cream parlor, Rebecca turned to Barry and smiled. She said, "When we get in here you can have anything you want."

"Really?" Barry perked up.

"Yes. Do you have anything in mind?"

"Could we share a banana split?"

It was just as Rebecca thought. Barry had a very shallow threshold for remorse.

102

Inside the brightly decorated ice cream parlor there were few patrons. An elderly couple sat side by side eating dipped cones and one other girl, who couldn't have been more than nineteen years old, sat alone with a double scoop of mint chocolate chip she worked on, content and perfectly oblivious to her surroundings. Rebecca and Barry approached the counter and placed their order to a young man whose face was pocked with acne. He wore a pink and white apron and silly hat that somewhat amused Rebecca.

When they found a seat, and waited for their order, Barry sat next to Rebecca in the booth and slid as close to her as he could get. He reached over and held her hand. His was tiny in Rebecca's small hand. Before she could speak, Barry said something that resounded with good intuition.

Barry said, "I know you understand me."

Rebecca pondered his words for a moment before the dessert arrived. When Barry took his first bite, Rebecca studied him. She asked, "What if I took care of you from now on? You and me. If I dealt with you as your parent instead of your mother, just me…we could have a lot of fun."

"Okay" Barry smiled his checkered grin.

Rebecca said, "You won't be going back to public school again."

Barry furrowed his brow. He asked, "Why not?"

"Baby, I think you know why. You don't play well with others and I don't think you were meant to."

"What about friends? How am I going to get any?"

"You have Sterling. He's your friend, right?"

"Well, yeah."

"Baby, you don't need a lot of friends. They can hold you back and one day you'll see that. For now, you've got to trust me. Do you trust me?"

"Yeah. I do."

"Beautiful. Let's finish our treat."

103

When Grace and the girls left the hospital, everyone was quiet. Mila rode in back with Darla and Grace could see in the rear-view mirror that the young girl was visibly upset. It was understandable and Grace worried about Darla, too. Darla had refused to go to school in the morning without Barry and she showed a defiant streak. Grace wasn't sure how she could make her go. When they had tried, Darla laid on the floor as stiff as a board and yelled out obscenities. Grace didn't know that her daughter knew the types of words she was yelling or if Darla understood what they meant. She did know that she couldn't send her to school to spew them at people and protest in public.

Mila came to stay with Grace for the day and Darla wanted to go with Barry. The family unit felt chaotic for Mila and she couldn't rid herself of negative thoughts. When Trey and Grace sat with Mila for lunch, Grace wanted to talk to Mila about the current situation. She wasn't sure how to go about the conversation.

Grace asked, "How do you feel, Mila?"

Mila prodded at the loaded, store-bought salad in front of her and pouted her lips. She said, "I don't know how I'm supposed to feel, but I guess I feel betrayed. My mommy tried to abandon me again."

Trey said, "It's alright to feel that way. Is there anything we can do to help you?"

Mila contemplated and shook her head. She said, "I just don't want to think about it. I'm trying not to. Maybe we can watch a movie?"

Grace asked, "What movie do you want to watch?"

Mila's eyes brimmed with tears. She said, "Sound of Music. It was my daddy's favorite."

Trey said, "You bet. We'll pick it up right after lunch."

Barry and Darla sat together in his room rolling cars on the floor. Darla watched him closely. She wondered how he could be taking what his mother did so well. She knew if her mom was in the hospital she would be upset. Darla didn't know exactly what was going on, only that Chloe hurt herself. Barry didn't seem to have a care in the world and it amazed her

Darla asked, "How did your mommy hurt herself?"

"She did it to herself. It wasn't my fault."

Darla thought his answer was strange. She couldn't comprehend what he meant. She asked, "Aren't you sad?"

"I don't get sad about most things."

"What if I got hurt? Would you be sad? Even if it wasn't your fault?"

Barry laughed. He said, "My momma doesn't love me. It's different."

"You think I love you?"

Barry furrowed his brow. He asked, "Don't you?"

"Yeah. I do."

"See. It's different."

Darla twisted a strand of hair around her finger and pouted her lips. She asked, "Don't you love your mommy?"

"I don't know." Barry crashed his toy car into one of the others and smiled.

Darla asked, "Do you love me?"

Barry threw himself back on the floor and groaned. He said, "Why do you ask me this stuff. It's annoying me."

"Well, do you?"

Barry sat up and put his hands on his head. He said, "I do, but I don't have to say it. Can we play cars?"

Darla stood and cocked her head to the side. She said, "You should at least be worried about your mom."

"Becca is my mom. My momma doesn't want me, so I'm not gonna worry about her."

Darla said, "I'm gonna take a nap. You make me tired."

Barry started rolling one of his toy cars back and forth. He said, "I know you think I don't feel, but I do."

"What's that supposed to mean?"

"Just what I said. I'm not a monster."

"I didn't say that. You just make me think too much and I'm tired."

Barry tried to imitate Darla's voice. He said, "I'm tired."

"Stop it. I'm not a baby."

"That's what you sound like."

"You're trying to be mean now."

"No, I'm not."

Darla left the room and went to the guest room where she took naps in the main house. Barry continued playing with his cars with a grin on his face.

104

Chloe was admitted to the psych ward and she didn't like the company of the other patients. Most of them had severe mental disturbances in the observation area. All the doctors and nurses clamored behind the see-through glass wall and the only form of entertainment was a single television that happened to be playing westerns. Not that there was anything wrong with that. She just couldn't concentrate on anything other than her own thoughts and guilt and westerns happened to be Peter's favorite type of television program. Something about the old shows pleased him, and having them play in the mental ward while she tried not to think of things that depressed her was a conundrum.

The woman in the recliner next to Chloe's smelled like vomit, but the observation room was full and there was nowhere to move to. It was comforting to Chloe to know that in seventy-two hours she could be going home. She felt groggy from the pills she had to take to satisfy the doctors. The smell of urine emanated from somewhere in the room. That with the smells of vomit and feces made it difficult for Chloe to cope with being trapped in one place. Being in a closed and locked setting where people moaned and groaned while defecating and pissing themselves felt suffocating.

When it came time to eat, Chloe only partook so that the people on staff didn't mark anything down that might negatively affect her prospects of going home. The meal could have been better for Chloe's taste, but she had put herself in the position she was in, with no one to complain to and nothing to be done about it. Chloe wondered what everyone was doing at home. She felt saddened inside that she couldn't cook dinner for the family. That she had made things the way they were. Maybe they were right. Maybe she was clinically depressed. Revisiting Peter's death and the man she murdered by accident did plague her.

A nurse approached Chloe with a plastic cup of pills and a paper cup of water. It seemed that they wanted to sedate her more than they wanted to observe her, but sleep was welcoming. The sleep the pills gave her was a peaceful one, with no dreams that Chloe could remember. She didn't like to remember her dreams, they were seldom good.

Dozing off this time, she did dream. She lay in a bed with Peter, just staring at him, watching him sleep. One of her favorite times to look at Peter was when he was sleeping because of how peaceful he looked and she could drink in every detail of his face at her leisure. Peter opened his eyes, and something in them was unsettling. They looked lifeless, like they were considering an abyss, straight through her.

Chloe asked, "Peter? Are you okay?"

Peter said, "I'm dead, Chloe. You have to let me go."

Peter began to decay rapidly and Chloe couldn't look away. It was as if she were frozen in place and as his face deteriorated, she felt panic welling up inside her and could hear her own breathing. Then she felt suspended in darkness, unable to wake herself but conscious of the room around her and the yelling of a patient. Abruptly her eyes opened and she could see the room again. Patients milling around and a distraught girl in the corner yelling that Satan had raped her. The orderlies rushed to the girl and she was ushered away and out of sight.

Being in the mental hospital with Peter on her mind and dreams of him telling her to let go disturbed her. She knew that Rebecca deserved more from her. The thought of Barry infuriated her. Mila visiting depressed her, because she had thus far attempted to abandon everyone who loves her and everyone she loves with a weak act of suicide that had failed miserably. It would be difficult to move past this incident and everything that had transpired in her life up to the point of it, but she knew that if she didn't, the suffering would never end.

105

Trey and Grace sat with Mila and talked about how life could be unpredictable. Mila had insight for someone her age. She said, "We can't stop the tide."

Trey asked, "Where did you hear that?"

"My mommy said it to me in Cancun. She said that the things that happen randomly in our lives are like the rolling tide. We just can't stop it no matter how much we try. It will keep rolling in and rolling out. She said that what happened with my daddy was like the tide."

Grace said, "It won't always be bad, though."

"I know that, Aunt Gracie. Things were getting good until this. I wish my brother wouldn't do things that cause us so many problems."

Grace said, "You know he's just protective. He was defending you from that bully before your father was shot and he was defending Darla when he got in trouble this last time. You can hardly blame him for that."

"Yeah, but he's evil, Aunt Gracie. I've seen it."

"He's your brother, short stuff. You don't want to stop loving your brother, do you?"

"I'm not saying that. I just know it will never end with him. It'll always be something."

106

Noma prepared the evening meal and Rebecca sat at the kitchen island watching her sway to the classical music that played on the home's stereo speakers. Young people always amazed Rebecca, especially one so full of life. An idea formed in Rebecca's mind about Noma. She contemplated the thought before speaking.

Rebecca asked, "Would you like to stay on with the family after you graduate college, Noma?"

Noma turned from her task at the oven. She asked, "For how long? I'll be in college for at least four more years. Maybe a lot longer. I was just planning on getting my bachelors degree at this one then going to a bigger one somewhere kind of far away after that."

"Interesting. Couldn't you get your masters here?"

"Yes. I could. I just want to travel a little and see things. Meet people, you know?"

"Baby, if you stay on with us you will have all benefits and I will pay for you to go places and see the world if you want. I need to know Barry will have someone stable in his life besides me."

"What about Chloe? She'll be home soon. He has both of you. Besides, don't you think you'll get tired of me? I don't cook all that great and I'm probably not the best influence all the time."

"You know, I don't know any people who are consistently good influences. If you sign a ten-year contract I will double your pay now and we will write in a certain amount of all expense paid vacations a year. I'm thinking two. One that you can bring Barry on and that we all might go on, then one in the summer to the destination of your choice, alone."

"Wow, Ms. Frost. That sounds amazing. Are you messing with me? It wouldn't be very nice. I'm sensitive."

"I'm not *messing* with you, Noma Rae Johnson. How many times have I asked you to call me Rebecca or Becca?"

"I'm sorry. All the talk about money makes me nervous. If you make a contract, I'll look it over. Is that okay?"

"That's perfectly fine."

Noma smiled and continued preparing the meal. With her back to Rebecca she mumbled. She said, "I would fuck you."

Rebecca asked, "Excuse me?"

Noma froze up. She turned and her cheeks were as red as cherry's. She asked, "Did you hear that?"

Rebecca said, "I heard. What did you mean?"

"I'm embarrassed. It was stupid. Just how you make me feel. I get hot when I talk to you sometimes. I just mumbled I didn't mean for you to hear."

Rebecca raised an eyebrow. She said, "Baby, I'm in no short supply of people who want to fuck me in all kinds of ways. Finish cooking and we'll talk later. About your promotion. Not fucking."

"Okay, Becca. I'm sorry." The embarrassed girl turned and Rebecca exited the kitchen.

107

Rebecca sat at her desk in the office of the house with the door locked. She played video from the move that Stephen helped Sandra with. Fast forwarding past the movers she could see Sandra and Stephen in the living room. The tape zoomed by in high speed until the two kissed. She watched to see where it would go and when Sandra produced a condom and helped put it on Stephen with her mouth, Rebecca stopped the tape and sat back in her chair.

Stephen knew that a likely consequence for having relations with anyone unapproved could result in his death, so the act was in blatant violation of the bond. Sandra had also been warned that he was hands off. She wouldn't be killed, but Rebecca thought that she should be cut off in the very least. Although Rebecca could overlook the incident altogether, she could not likely forgive the unloyalty from either of them. She picked up the phone to call Stephen.

When he answered, Rebecca asked, "How did the move go with Sandra?"

"It went fine, boss. She's all settled in."

"You know, she's a loose one like I said. Did she give

you any grief? Try to come on to you?"

"No. Nothing like that."

"Alright. I'll have you over later. Be here at eight o'clock. Come in through the veranda."

"I planned on having dinner there. Unless you want me to wait for Chloe to come home."

"Yes, well. I think you should skip dinner."

"Is there something wrong?"

"Baby, there's always something wrong. My head is just messed up right now with everything and I don't feel like doing the dinner with the family tonight."

"Okay, boss. I'll be there at eight o'clock."

Rebecca sat down her phone and thought about Chloe. She imagined that losing Stephen might be another hard blow for Chloe because she had grown attached to him. She wasn't exactly sure how she would proceed, but she thought that killing Stephen might be a bad idea at this stage.

Her cell phone rang with an unfamiliar number. Rebecca answered and it was Chloe from the hospital, her voice meek and low like she had been crying. Rebecca asked, "What's wrong, baby?"

Chloe said, "I want to come home. I hate this place."

"Baby, you know you have to stay. Just a couple of more days and you can come home."

"I want to come home now. Does Stephen know I'm in here?"

"He knows, baby."

"It's so embarrassing. Do you think he'll look at me the same?"

"Don't worry, baby. Stephen won't look at you any differently."

"Why hasn't he visited me?"

"Do you want him to?"

"I'd like a visit. I thought he cared about me."

"I'm sure he cares for you very much. I'll call him and tell him that you want to see him."

"You'll do that?"

"Yes, baby. I'll do it as soon as we hang up."

"Thank you, Becca. I love you so much. I'm sorry I'm weak."

"You're not weak, baby. You just had a moment of weakness. We all do." Saying the words, Rebecca knew that her next moment of weakness would be letting Stephen live.

She redialed Stephen. She said, "Go visit Chloe at the hospital at seven o'clock. When you're finished with your visit, come see me."

"Okay, boss. I'll be there."

Rebecca wasn't pleased with the turn of events, but she had to think about damage control. Ripping someone else from Chloe's life could be devastating and she didn't want to add to her lover's grief. It could turn out to be a complicated task and Rebecca smiled to herself as possible ideas formed. There had to be a price to pay.

108

Hand in hand, Chloe and Stephen sat in silence. She leaned her head on his shoulder and he could feel she was shaking. He reached up and smoothed her hair. Being in the place she was in Stephen could understand her anxiety. He observed the surroundings with contempt.

He said, "You should be out of here in two days, right?"

"Yeah. That's what they say. I wish we could visit in a private room. I don't know why we have to sit out here with everyone."

A lady with stringy grey hair approached them and stood staring at them with beady dark and glassy eyes. She said, "Repent and you can be saved. Judgment day is coming! Say you repent in Jesus' name."

When she got loud one of the orderlies came to usher her to her room. Chloe said, "I'm not like these people."

Stephen placed his fingers below her chin and lifted so that her light blue eyes met his. Chloe considered Stephen's hazel eyes and became curious of how he managed to become property of Rebecca. Stephen smiled showing his big white teeth. He looked like a handsome wolf to Chloe.

Stephen said, "Try not to let this place get you down. When you come home I'll give you a nice massage if you want."

Chloe bit her lip. She said, "I'd like that."

She turned her head and looked away. She spoke in a soft almost inaudible tone. She asked, "Do you see me differently now?"

Stephen squeezed her hand and moved in close to her ear. He said, "You're hurt inside. We all see you as the beautiful person you are."

Chloe tried not to smile, but she couldn't stop herself. She turned and kissed Stephen softly, then the orderly walked over to let them know that visitation was over. Chloe hugged Stephen and watched him leave. Tears rose in her eyes. She wondered if she would ever be able to forgive herself for her moment of weakness. Everyone else seemed to love her the same and it was almost unbearable. She liked that no one shunned her, but she almost wished someone would just cuss her out for being the fool she had been.

109

The room was dimly lit and Rebecca sipped wine and watched as Stephen undressed. She asked, "Have you been sleeping with other people, Stephen?"

Stephen paused removing his pants, then continued to undress. He said, "I know not to do that."

"Baby, you don't have to lie to me."

"I know what could happen if I slept with someone you didn't approve. I wouldn't admit to it if I did."

Rebecca produced a silenced .380. She said, "Stand up straight so that I can look at you."

Stephen did as he was told and could see the killer's gleam. Like a predator about to take down her prey. Someone with as many kills as Rebecca had no doubt thoroughly enjoyed her work. Taking another human's life meant little to her and at the slightest disrespect or threat she would take the life of someone who opposed her. Stephen knew better than to try to defend himself in the situation. The accuracy and speed of Rebecca's kills were always on point. From where he stood, Stephen was already a dead man. Naked with nowhere to go in a sound proof room where no one could hear at the mercy of the one who had the right within the organization to kill him if she so much as pleased to.

Rebecca said, "Get on your knees."

Stephen slowly went to his knees and watched Rebecca stand and casually approach him. Rebecca thought to herself that she should go ahead and end his life. Letting him live for Chloe's sake didn't settle well with her. Stephen closed his eyes and Rebecca put her suppressor against his left eyelid.

She said, "You should be dead right now. I'm going to let you live today, but if I find out you have gone outside of our relationship any time from this day forward there will be no other consequence than death. Do you like Chloe?"

"I do."

"Beautiful. You should be satisfied with the both of us. I'm going to give you a single opportunity now. You can renew your life vow to me here and now and you can go on with us, or you can leave now and never return. This is your opportunity to be free of your obligation. You will be banished from the organization and may never attempt to approach me or Chloe again, or renew your vow."

"I would like to renew my vow."

Rebecca said, "Kiss my feet."

He knew she would not have let him live if he didn't renew his vow, but it was her way. Now that he did, there was no turning back and if she ever caught him cheating again she would not be able to overlook it. Just knowing he had already defied her could be an unforgivable crime so letting him live was an act of mercy, although if anyone knew it was for Chloe she knew it would look like weakness. If she could bury Sandra and him both in unmarked graves without having to deal with a whole new mess now, she would.

110

When Sandra came home from the dry cleaners where Rebecca had gotten her a job, she was surprised to find Rebecca in her apartment. Sandra asked, "What are you doing here? Who let you in?"

"I let myself in. I own this complex. It's not hard for me to get a key."

"Is there some reason for your visit?"

Rebecca raised her eyebrow. She said, "There is. Why else would I be here? I have my own place."

"You're acting strange."

"Interesting. I found out that the man I sent to visit you was in this very apartment that I gave you for a long period. What happened?"

Sandra tapped her foot and looked annoyed. Rebecca shook her head and laughed. She said, "Don't start that again, Sandy. You know how it will end if you get testy with me."

"You're the one trespassing. Whether you own this apartment complex or not, you can't just barge in on tenants."

"You know, if that's the way you want to play this game, I play viciously and with a passion. You put in an order for the stove to be replaced, didn't you?"

"I did. What does that have to do with anything?"

"I came to check on the stove before my manager approved the repairs and found these drugs on the table." Rebecca produced a bag of powder cocaine. "Looks like an eight ball to me. What is it?"

"I don't know what that is."

"You do cocaine, though. I happen to know from a reliable source."

"You can't prove that's mine."

"Interesting. You want to see how far I'll push this? I want you out of my apartment complex and my life by the weekend or I'll make sure you have a really rough go of things, worse than you can imagine."

"Look, Rebecca, I wouldn't jeopardize what I have going with you for some guy. That's what this is about, right?"

"Baby, this is about cocaine." Rebecca threw the bag on the table.

"That's not mine."

"If you don't want it flush it. I've got pictures of it and had a witness with me when I came in, took pictures of it and everything. You're being evicted. You can save a lengthy process and move by the end of the week, or you can face prosecution. There's no telling where you might have dropped a baggy. I'm sure you could be sloppy enough to leave them all over the place. We have a zero-tolerance policy here and you're in violation."

Sandra began to cry. She said, "Please, Rebecca. I have nowhere to go."

"Go to a shelter or live under a bridge for all I care. I'm done."

When Rebecca left the apartment, she smiled to herself. Sandra would likely try to snort the contents of the bag and be in la-la land. Then she would be out of the picture for good. The camera had been removed and there would be no witness to the death but the sheet rock.

111

The day Chloe was released from the hospital Rebecca walked her out and they climbed into the Lexus smiling. Chloe felt ecstatic, she imagined that what she was feeling must be what someone being released from prison must feel like. Her smile faded as she thought that one day Elvin Craig would be released. She thought he should have gotten the death penalty for gunning Peter down. Rebecca noticed her sudden solemnness.

Rebecca asked, "What are you thinking about, baby?"

Chloe shook her head and bit her lip. She said, "I don't want to talk about it now. Can we get cheeseburgers?"

"Baby, you can have anything you want. The world is yours."

Chloe smiled. She said, "I love you, Becca."

"I love you, too, baby. Let's get some cheeseburgers. I know the perfect place."

After their meal, Rebecca smiled at Chloe. She said, "Baby, I think you're going to be just fine. There's something I want to talk to you about."

Chloe bit her lip and started fidgeting. She asked, "Is it bad?"

"No. I don't think it is, baby. I know you've become attached to Stephen and I've asked him to move into the house. He'll be in one of the guest rooms upstairs. Is that okay?"

Chloe smiled and then rolled her eyes. She said, "You scared me. I thought it was going to be something bad. Of course, I don't mind."

Rebecca raised her eyebrow and smirked. She said, "I didn't think you would, but you're my wife, we have to run things past each other."

"I'm ready to be home. Can we leave now?"

"Interesting. No chocolate shake?"

"I'm stuffed, Becca."

"Beautiful. The children are waiting to see you."

Chloe cringed and Rebecca frowned. Rebecca asked, "What's wrong? You do want to see the children, don't you?"

"I don't want to see Barry."

"Barry isn't there, baby. He's with Griffin and Sterling. It's just the girls."

"Okay. I'm sorry. After what I did I feel like it's going to be hard to look at Barry again."

"Eventually you must face him. We're all going to be living under the same roof, nothing has changed. Part of the reason that Stephen is moving in is so Barry will have a male role model in the house. You won't have to deal with the boy, I'll hold up my promise and assume all responsibility for him. Baby, just be strong and try to move past that day."

"I will, Becca. I don't mean to be this way." Chloe

began to fidget.

Rebecca said, "Baby, none of us mean to be the way we are most of the time. We're human and you have to believe me when I tell you that everything will be alright."

Chloe bit her lip and looked Rebecca in the eyes. She said, "I believe you."

"Beautiful. Let's hit the road."

112

Rebecca knew that the situation was still volatile and that a decision from the council could tilt the scale in either direction regarding Chloe's life. She did well to hide her concern and felt anxious inside to hear the verdict. When they pulled up to the house, the whole family was in the front yard waiting and seeing all of them together and knowing how much they cared for Chloe sparked a pain in Rebecca's chest she hadn't felt before. It would almost be too much to bear if she lost Chloe now. She had resisted the urge to call Griffin over the last couple of days while she waited to hear the conclusion.

Chloe stepped out of the car and Mila rushed to her wrapping her arms around her mother. After the group went into the house all the adults had tall glasses of wine poured and the children had juice. They sat in the living room and talked about their lives, never mentioning the reason for Chloe's absence in the past week. Mila and Noma were the most talkative.

Noma said, "Oh, I have to tell you. Me and James are going steady now. He said I'm his girl and everything. And Ms. Becca had me sign a ten year contract. So I'm going to be on for a long time now and I can renew when it's up. I'm so excited it's like having a whole 'nother family. We really missed you here. I don't cook like you, but everybody's been nice enough to eat my dinners anyway." Noma laughed.

Mila said, "Gabby's mom won't let her come over anymore." She pouted.

Chloe asked, "Why not?"

Mila said, "Heck. I don't know. Her mom is mad at mom and now she won't let Gabby come over. Gabby says that when she's with her dad he'll let her come over, but that her mom still tries to tell her dad what to do even though they're divorced."

Rebecca said, "Interesting. She thinks it's okay to get back at an adult during a feud through the children. It's childish and irresponsible."

Mila asked, "Can't you make up with her, Mom? I really want to see Gabby."

"Baby, I'll see what I can do. For now, let's just enjoy the evening with your mommy. We'll worry about other people later."

"Yes, ma'am."

Chloe asked, "Have you been going to school, Mila?"

"Yes, that's where I see Gabby."

Grace said, "This one hasn't been going." She pointed to Darla.

Darla said, "I don't want to go to school. I want to be homeschooled here. You can't make me go."

Grace said, "You watch that attitude, little missy. Simmer it down before you get yourself in the hot pot. I told you we're thinking about it."

Trey said, "We're getting ready to head to the house. I thought Stephen was going to be over. We've got to go run errands and get cleaned up, then we'll be back for dinner."

Chloe said, "Good because I'm going to make fried chicken with all the sides."

Grace groaned. She said, "You bet we'll be back. Now my mouth is going to be watering the whole time we're gone."

The front door opened and Stephen found them all in the living room. Trey said, "There he is. Man, are you going to come help me build the deck this weekend, or what?"

"Dude, you know I'm down. You're buying the beer, right?"

"Beer and barbecue, just like we planned. I mean, if Chloe's up to it."

The men looked at Chloe with question in their eyes. Chloe said, "I'm not about to spoil the boy's day, I'll be there, if I don't have to help with the deck." She laughed.

Stephen said, "Darling, you don't have to do a thing. We can talk about it more later if you want."

Rebecca amused herself watching Stephen interact with everyone, especially Chloe. She thought to herself that they really did have a family going and that sometimes when it comes to family it's okay to forgive errors. She felt relieved she hadn't killed Stephen. Although, deep inside, she thought that it could be a mistake, seeing the way Chloe looked at him made the difference.

113

When the weekend came, Chloe went to Stephen's room and plopped down on his bed while he sat busy at the computer. He told her that he ran online stores for the organization, and she wondered if there was more to it. She suspected he did some kind of covert black market stuff. When he finished typing he turned in his chair and smiled his dazzling smile.

He said, "You about ready to go?"

Chloe rolled her eyes. She said, "Everyone's ready except you."

He laughed. He said, "I'm ready, but the way you're looking at me says you aren't exactly ready, darling. Anything I can do?"

"You can climb on this bed with me and show me what you're made of."

"Is that right? While everyone waits?"

"Don't tell me you don't like being bad." Chloe started unbuttoning her blouse. She said, "I know you aren't going to deny me."

Stephen stood and pulled his shirt off, throwing it to the floor. He said, "No, ma'am. I'm at your service."

With all the grief that Chloe had gone through, she

was learning to enjoy life again and move forward. Although she would never forget Peter, she knew that if she was going to get better she would have to let go of her grief and embrace her new life. Having everyone close that cared for her and being with Rebecca and Stephen eased her suffering, and when Stephen climbed into the bed with her she released her inhibitions and submitted to feeling the passion of a man.

114

The Barker home bustled with life. Noma, Grace, Chloe and Rebecca sat in lawn chairs and watched the children play and the men work. They sipped margaritas and laughed amongst themselves while Noma told unsavory jokes mainly having to do with genitals. The girl's sense of humor could be considered somewhat perverted, but the women enjoyed her company.

Rebecca said, "Noma, I don't know where you come up with all of this, but you are hilarious."

Noma said, "I can't help it. I think cock and balls are funny."

Chloe said, "Sweetie they are funny, but I think you might be obsessed."

Griffin called Rebecca from outside the residence. Barry had invited Sterling to the cookout and Griffin wanted to be let in. Rebecca made her way through the house and met him at the front door. She said, "You could have just walked in."

Griffin let Sterling run in to find the rest of the children. He said, "I thought dis would be a good way for us to get a word together."

Rebecca's interest piqued. She said, "Let's go to the

garage."

Once in the garage Griffin whistled. He said, "What's dis? Looks like a sixty-eight drop top Camaro. A fuckin' mint."

"You know that Trey has a thing for classics, we're not here to talk about cars."

"Yeah, but look at dis beast. Cowl hood, candy blue paint, chrome for days. He must of paid some major stacks for those wheels, too. Look like they at least some twennies. My man knows how it's done."

"Are you trying to aggravate me now?"

"Naw, boss. You know I'm jus' sayin'. Anyway, it's not bad news. The council voted to stay. Your girl ain't in no danger."

A pressure from deep within Rebecca subsided. She said, "Thank you, Griffin. She's really a good girl. She won't go astray."

"I believe it, boss. That's what I told 'em. She can't do that shit again, though. If they think she's weak and might break they say she too close in to be that unstable. It's all good for now, but she has to get her shit together."

"Beautiful. Let me worry about that. I'll make sure she's stable and there won't be anything like this happening again."

"Dat's good, boss. Another thing. Sandra called me the other day and said you left dope at her place, wanted me to help her move. Wanted to come stay with me. I told her she should flush the dope and move, but she couldn't stay with me. I know there was probably some sick shit in that bag. She's a slut, boss, but she got that little girl. I don't think she should die. So, since I did this for you, you could do that for me. She don't know nothin'."

"Alright. I'll let her live, but she better not make any more problems for me."

"I can't vouch that she won't, but for now give 'er a pass."

When they left the garage, Rebecca's mood was lighter than it had been since Chloe's attempt at suicide. The mystery of why Sandra hadn't died the night she left the laced bag of cocaine in front of her had been solved and Chloe was in the clear. She sat in her lawn chair with the other women with a smile that wouldn't leave her face. Chloe reached over and grasped her hand.

Rebecca said, "Ladies, this is the good life."

Griffin joined the men to help build the deck and everything seemed like it was just as it should be for the moment.

Chloe said, "It sure is."

TO BE CONTINUED …

DON'T MISS THE NEXT INSTALLMENT IN THE UGLINESS TRILOGY!

Book Three: The Culmination

Scheduled for release in January, 2019

THE CULMINATION

PREVIEW

CHAPTER 1

In the weeks after Chloe's attempted suicide, the odd little family had become closer and the relationship between Chloe, Rebecca and Stephen had become something that, although strange, everyone accepted. Grace sat with Noma in the chaise lounge by the pool soaking up the sunshine while Barry, Mila, Darla and Gabby splashed and made a ruckus. Stephen and Trey were by the grill tending the meat and drinking beers. No one talked about the suicide attempt or the love triangle openly.

Chloe spent a lot of time in the bedroom, and on some of those days when she didn't feel confident enough to face anyone, Stephen would come and talk to her, or Rebecca would watch movies with her. She knew that everyone tried to do what she wanted and make her happy. The difficult thing about her situation was that she knew that no one could actually know or feel the way that she felt, except maybe Mila. Only she and Mila really knew how good of a man Peter had been and what he had meant to them.

Barry wasn't the type to feel much of anything, and now that Rebecca and Stephen were taking on all the responsibilities of raising him, Chloe's life became easier—but when she saw Barry, she could feel a blind fury build and boil within herself. Some of her worst thoughts came in his presence and there didn't seem to be an escape.

Rebecca wore a black teddy that didn't cover much and sat in one of the armchairs in the corner of the room, looking at Chloe. She said, "Baby, I've got to go on one of my trips this weekend. Are you going to be okay here?"

Chloe rolled her eyes. She asked, "Why wouldn't I be? I'm a big girl."

"You know. I don't like to think that you would do anything foolish. It's hard for my mind not to wander."

"I know what you mean, Becca. You think just because I had a moment of weakness, that I might try to kill myself again. I can promise you that isn't going to happen. I'm not going out like that. I'm staying right here with your sexy ass as long as I can."

Rebecca stood and turned, leaning over the chair. She asked, "Do you really think my ass is sexy?"

Chloe bit her lip. She said, "You need to stop. Get over here."

Rebecca crossed the room and climbed into bed with Chloe. When they began to kiss, Chloe's skin heated and the hairs on her arms stood erect. She could feel passion running through her veins. Rebecca pushed herself back and considered Chloe's eyes. She could see the fire of desire burning with an animalistic quality.

Rebecca said, "I think you need to go out with the family more. You've been locking yourself up in this room too much."

Chloe huffed and rolled her eyes. She said, "This is the perfect time to chastise me, Becca. You know you had me going."

"Baby, I'm serious. You can't avoid everyone forever. You're going to have to blend back into the family eventually."

"There's plenty of time for that, Becca. I'm not going to become a hermit if that's what you're worried about."

"It's not that, baby. I just want you to be happy and healthy."

Chloe bit her lip and smirked. She said, "I am happy and healthy. Come closer."

"I don't think so. You need to at least tell me you will try to spend more time out of this room while I'm away."

"I will, Becca. Kiss me."

Rebecca leaned in and locked lips with Chloe. Just like that, the spark reignited and the pace quickened in a hurry. Both women breathed as one, and for the moment there were no others in the world, only the two with bodies intertwined. Chloe wished she could live suspended with that feeling of pleasure forever and forget all her worries, but she knew that Rebecca's words rang true. She would have to become a part of the family again.

When the frenzy calmed, Rebecca raised her eyebrow and shook her head. She said, "It's hard to believe that we're here together. I had planned on seducing you for a fling when we first met. Now look at us. We're a family. You're my wife."

"It is hard to believe, Becca. I just wish you would quit talking and give me what you know I want."

"You know. I could get dressed and join everyone outside."

"You wouldn't."

"I would. But not before I give you that O you've been anticipating. Then we're both going outside."

"It's a deal."

~o~